Rahul Singh

PSYCHOWRATH

Psychowrath

Rahul Singh

PSYCHOWRATH

The Story of a Psychopath beyond imagination

RAHUL SINGH

Psychowrath

This is a work of fiction. All characters, organizations and events in this publication are either products of the author's imagination or are used fictitiously, and any resemblance to real persons, living or dead, is purely coincidental.

If you'd like to get in touch, I'd love to hear from you! You can reach me through the following channels:
Email: rahulsingh97293@gmail.com
Instagram: rahulsingh86828
LinkedIn: www.linkedin.com/in/rahul-singh8

Rahul Singh

CONTENTS

Love is a game of thorns. Play at your own risk.

~Author

Chapter One: The Farewell

Friendship, they say, stands the test of hardship. But what about a love so potent it transforms a friend into a devil in disguise, willing to pay any price for affection?

Born into a middle-class family, Anesh always seemed like a bright boy. As his name suggests, he was a brilliant student in his class. Anesh's life had always been a quiet study in contrasts.

On one hand, there was his father, hardworking and honest folk who valued education more than anything else. Their modest home bustled with the comforting routines of a typical middle-class family – shared meals, hurried goodbyes, and the ever-present hum of the television in the evenings.

Anesh, ever the obedient son, thrived in this environment. He excelled in his studies, consistently topping his class with an almost effortless brilliance.

They lived in the small town of Kasauli, a hill station nestled amidst the verdant embrace of the Himalayas in India. The air hung crisp and clean, perpetually scented with the sweet fragrance of pine. Winding roads snaked through the town, offering breathtaking glimpses of the valleys below.

Psychowrath

Kasauli's charm resided not just in its picturesque beauty, but also in its peaceful tranquility – a perfect backdrop for the quiet rhythm of their lives.

Growing up as an only child, Anesh craved companionship. Luckily, fate intervened when he met Ishank.

Unlike Anesh, who hailed from a small, quiet family, Ishank came from a rich household. Ishank, with his easy smile and infectious enthusiasm, was a breath of fresh air for Anesh.

Their friendship blossomed quickly, not a fleeting connection, but a deep bond forged through countless games, shared secrets whispered under starry skies, and a fierce loyalty that ran deeper than their own backyards.

While Ishank wasn't as fond of books as Anesh, he had a warmth and unwavering support that perfectly balanced Anesh's studious focus. Anesh, ever the helpful friend, would patiently explain things whenever schoolwork left Ishank scratching his head.

After school, their backpacks slung over their shoulders, they'd race home, a whirlwind of laughter and friendly shoves. Reaching their doorsteps, the race would end in a tie, both breathless and grinning. Though a few houses apart, their homes felt like extensions of each other's. The aroma of Ishank's mom's delicious potato and cauliflower curry, a dish called Aloo Gobi, would often waft through the air, beckoning them over for steaming plates of comfort food.

In return, Anesh's house always had a fresh batch of Jalebis, those sweet, deep-fried twists dipped in syrup, waiting to satisfy their sweet tooth.

School was another adventure they tackled together. Sitting side-by-side in class, their elbows would brush as they scribbled furiously in notebooks. Sometimes, notes were exchanged, but more often, it was whispered jokes and silly doodles that filled the margins.

Dusty textbooks transformed into exciting tales with their imaginations running wild. History lessons became grand battles where they'd strategize like miniature generals, and science experiments turned into messy but thrilling explorations of the world around them.

Their bond was a shield against anyone who dared to disrupt their world. If a bully targeted one of them, the other would appear like a superhero, ready to defend their friend.

Anesh, with his fiery temper, would launch into a passionate defense, his voice rising in indignation. Ishank, the calmer of the two, would use his quick wit to de-escalate the situation, diffusing the tension with a well-timed joke or a clever quip. Together, they were an unbeatable force.

One scorching summer afternoon, a heated game of cricket was in full swing. A new student named Rohan, eager to prove himself, shoved Ishank, sending him sprawling in the dirt. Anesh, his face flushed with anger, marched towards Rohan, fists clenched tight. Before a fight could erupt, Ishank, brushing the dirt off his clothes, scrambled to his feet.

"Don't worry about it, Anesh," he said, his voice calm despite the tremor that ran through it. "It's not worth getting in trouble."

Anesh, however, wouldn't let it go. "But he had no right to push you!" he argued, his voice tight with anger.

Rohan, sensing the rising tension, scoffed. "So what? He was in my way anyway."

Ever the peacemaker, Ishank stepped forward, a hint of a smile playing on his lips. "Why don't we just finish the game?" he suggested. "Maybe Rohan can even join our team next time."

Rohan, taken aback by the unexpected offer, stammered, "B-but I don't really know how to play."

Anesh's anger melted away, replaced by a wide grin. "That's okay," he boomed, "we can teach you!"

And so, their little team grew. The initial spark of conflict transformed into a new friendship, a testament to the strength of their bond.

As the years rolled by, their friendship weathered many storms – arguments over borrowed comics, fights over who got the bigger slice of cake, and the occasional disagreement about homework. But through it all, their connection remained strong, a constant source of support and laughter.

Their academic years flowed by in a comfortable rhythm. Then, in the pivotal year of 10th grade, a new student named Ishita arrived, causing a ripple of excitement through their class.

Ishita possessed a beauty that defied easy description. Her eyes, the color of deep emeralds, held a quiet intelligence that sparkled with humor when she smiled. Her dark hair, a cascade of midnight silk, framed a face that seemed sculpted by the hand of an artist.

Even her movements held a captivating grace, a silent melody that drew attention without her needing to try. It wasn't just her physical features, though; there was a warmth to her smile, a genuine curiosity in her gaze that made her presence a beacon in the often-mundane classroom environment.

Psychowrath

The boys, of course, were immediately smitten. Whispers and stolen glances followed Ishita wherever she went. But for Anesh, a deeper feeling bloomed in his chest. He found himself captivated not just by her beauty, but by the air of quiet strength she carried. He loved her, silently for now, a secret melody playing only in the chambers of his heart.

Ishita, the new girl in class, navigated the unfamiliar faces with a quiet grace. Needing to catch up on missed lessons, she found herself drawn to the two students consistently at the top of the class: Anesh and Ishank. Tentatively, she approached them during lunch break, her voice barely a whisper as she asked if they could share their notes.

Anesh, ever the studious one, readily agreed, offering his meticulously organized notes with a shy smile. Ishank, the class clown, with a mischievous glint in his eyes, teased her playfully before offering his own colorful (and often slightly embellished) version of events.

Yet, despite their contrasting personalities, a connection sparked between them the day Ishank, in a fit of playful rebellion, accidentally launched a spitball that landed squarely on the back of Ishita's head.

Ishita, the girl in question, was a force of nature. With quick wit and a sharper tongue, she could dissect a bad joke with surgical precision or weave a captivating story from the most mundane details. When the rogue spitball struck, she whirled around, eyes blazing.

But instead of the expected fury, a flicker of amusement danced in their depths. Ishank, bracing himself for a verbal (or possibly physical) counterattack, was surprised by a mischievous grin mirroring his own.

"Nice shot," she quipped, her voice laced with playful sarcasm.

Anesh, usually swallowed by his own shyness, surprised everyone, including himself, by speaking up. "Actually," he offered, his voice barely a whisper, "it was an accident."

Ishank, ever the performer, threw his hands up in mock surrender. "Guilty as charged, your majesty! But in my defense, this projectile," he brandished the offending wad of paper with a flourish, "was clearly yearning for a taste of adventure."

The tension in the air dissipated, replaced by a burst of laughter. Ishita, unable to resist his theatrics, dissolved into giggles, tears welling in her own eyes.

Anesh, caught off guard by the unexpected turn of events, found himself smiling, a hesitant curve of his lips that crinkled the corners of his eyes.

Psychowrath

From that day on, an unlikely friendship blossomed. Lunch breaks became a shared affair, a refuge from the pressures of school and adolescence.

Ishank, the eternal jester, regaled them with tales of his latest escapades, each embellished with fantastical details that left Ishita snorting with laughter and Anesh shaking his head in mock disapproval. But beneath the playful barbs, a genuine connection grew. Ishank, for all his clowning, possessed a genuine warmth and a disarming honesty.

Anesh, usually reserved, found himself opening up, sharing his love for classic literature and his quiet anxieties about upcoming exams. Ishita, the bridge between them, wove their stories together with her insightful observations and witty commentary.

Their afternoons weren't just filled with laughter. After school, they migrated to the quiet solitude of the library, a haven of hushed whispers and the rhythmic scratching of pencils.

Ishank, surprisingly focused when the mood struck, would tackle his homework with renewed vigor, fueled by Ishita's sharp explanations and Anesh's patient tutoring.

Anesh, in turn, would be drawn out of his studious shell by Ishita's contagious enthusiasm, venturing beyond the textbook to explore the fascinating worlds hidden within the library's dusty shelves.

Weekends were for exploration. They'd spend lazy afternoons by the town lake, skipping stones across the shimmering water and sharing dreams for the future.

Ishank, with his boundless optimism, envisioned a life filled with adventure and laughter. Anesh, more practical, dreamt of a secure future built on academic success. Ishita, ever the realist, saw a blend of both in their futures, a tapestry woven from ambition, laughter, and the unwavering support of their newfound friendship.

As the months turned into years, their bond deepened. Through whispered secrets shared under a starlit sky and inside jokes that only they understood, they formed a safe haven, a world where they could be themselves without judgment.

Two years flew by in a whirlwind of late-night study sessions, the nervous thrill of school plays, and the muffled giggles of shared jokes during lunch.

Graduation, both a joyous celebration and a bittersweet goodbye to their high school days, loomed large on the horizon.

Anesh, ever the quiet observer, had harbored a secret affection for Ishita, a blossoming feeling nestled deep within him like a melody only his heart could hear.

Psychowrath

The farewell day arrived, a day tinged with a bittersweet mix of excitement for the future and a touch of sadness for the chapters ending.

The insistent buzz of his phone startled Anesh awake, pulling him from the comfortable haze of sleep. Squinting at the screen, he saw Ishank's name flashing, momentarily banishing the drowsiness.

"Hey Anesh, you up for the party tonight?" Ishank's voice crackled through the phone, laced with a familiar enthusiasm.

Anesh forced a smile, the sound strained even to his own ears. "Absolutely, wouldn't miss it for the world." A knot of guilt tightened in his stomach, a secret shame he couldn't bring himself to confess to his best friend.

"Awesome! We can head over together then," Ishank suggested, the excitement bubbling over in his voice.

"Actually," Anesh stammered, his mind scrambling for an excuse, "I might be a bit late. Something... kind of important came up."

There was a beat of silence on the other end of the line, a pause that felt heavy with unspoken questions.

"No worries, dude," Ishank finally replied, his voice laced with a hint of disappointment. "See you there." The call ended, leaving Anesh with a leaden weight settling in his gut.

The truth was the prospect of a celebratory party held little allure compared to the thought of seeing Ishita. His mind was a kaleidoscope of memories, each one a poignant reminder of the things left unsaid. He saw her smile in his mind's eye, the way her eyes crinkled at the corners when she laughed, a telltale sign of genuine amusement.

Every stolen glance, every whispered conversation they'd shared echoed in the cavernous halls of his memory, amplifying the regret that gnawed at him. He wished with a fervor that bordered on desperation that he'd spoken up, confessed the feelings that simmered beneath the surface of their friendship.

But Anesh, by nature, was a reserved soul. He navigated the world with a quiet intensity, his emotions kept tightly concealed. He excelled in academics, his mind a finely tuned machine that devoured information with insatiable hunger. Yet, when it came to matters of the heart, he fumbled, his carefully constructed facade crumbling in the face of vulnerability.

Confessing his feelings to Ishita, the girl who occupied a special place in his heart, felt like venturing into uncharted territory, a terrifying prospect that left him paralyzed with indecision.

The day stretched before him, an expanse of empty hours leading to the much-anticipated evening. Anesh found himself going through the motions, a hollow shell drifting through the familiar routines of his life. He endured breakfast with his parents, their excited chatter about his upcoming graduation a stark contrast to the turmoil within him.

As the day passed, Anesh felt increasingly anxious. The cheerful chatter and laughter around him only served to magnify the weight of his concerns. He desperately wanted to see Ishita and finally express his feelings, but his own uncertainty held him back.

Anesh took a deep breath, his heart hammering a frantic rhythm against his ribs. Tonight was the night. He'd held his feelings for Ishita captive within him for far too long, and with graduation looming on the horizon, it felt like his last chance.

With a rose and chocolates in hand, he steeled himself for Ishita. His gaze darted across the crowded room, searching for the girl who occupied his every thought. There she was, bathed in the warm glow of the fairy lights, her head thrown back in laughter as she conversed with Ishank by the punch bowl.

A wave of icy dread washed over him. They were together, closer than he'd ever dared to imagine. Ishank's hand rested casually on Ishita's waist, a gesture of possessiveness that sent a jolt of jealousy through Anesh. It couldn't be true, could it? Had they been keeping their feelings secret all this time? Was

Ishank, his best friend, the one who had stolen the girl of his dreams?

The world tilted on its axis, reality blurring at the edges. Betrayal, anger, and a crushing sense of loss threatened to drown him in a tidal wave of despair. He stood there, rooted to the spot, throwing the rose and chocolates in the dustbin, the scene replaying in his mind like a cruel film reel.

Suddenly, a hand landed on his shoulder, shattering the fragile hold he had on his emotions. It was Ishank.

"Anesh, man! Where have you been hiding? We thought you weren't coming," boomed Ishank, completely oblivious to the emotional storm raging within his friend.

Anesh forced a smile, the gesture feeling brittle and unconvincing even to himself. "Just not feeling too well," he rasped, his voice barely a whisper.

He retreated to a secluded corner; the taste of ashes heavy on his tongue. The night stretched before him, an agonizing eternity filled with forced conversations and hollow laughter.

Ishita and Ishank seemed to be joined at the hip, their easy camaraderie a constant reminder of the distance that separated him from Ishita. Every stolen glance, every shared joke they exchanged felt like a dagger to his heart.

The night stretched before him like an endless, agonizing tunnel. Forced conversations and hollow laughter filled the air, but none of it registered with him. Ishita and Ishank were inseparable, their easy friendship a constant reminder of the chasm that had opened between him and Ishita. Every stolen glance, every shared joke they exchanged, felt like a tiny knife twisting in his heart.

He couldn't tear his eyes away from them. Their happiness was a cruel reflection of his misery. A tightness constricted his chest, making it hard to breathe. An announcement boomed through the microphone, shattering the fragile bubble of his despair.

"And now, the highlight of the evening! Ishank and Ishita will grace us with a beautiful dance!"

Anesh's blood seemed to turn to molten lava. He watched, numb with a kind of horrible fascination, as they walked together towards the stage. The spotlight bathed them in a warm glow, illuminating the smiles on their faces.

The music started, a slow, romantic melody. Ishank placed a hand on Ishita's waist, his eyes filled with a tenderness that made Anesh clench his fists. Ishita leaned into his touch, a shy blush creeping up her cheeks.

They moved together as if they were one, their bodies swaying in perfect harmony. It was a dance of unspoken emotions, a story told without words. Anesh saw a connection he could never hope to replicate, a bond forged in shared experiences and deep understanding.

With each graceful turn and dip, a fresh wave of jealousy washed over him. He remembered the countless times he had dreamt of dancing with Ishita, of holding her close and whispering sweet nothings in her ear. But those dreams had turned to dust, scattered by the harsh reality of his own insecurities and Ishank's genuine affection for her.

As the music reached its crescendo, Ishank twirled Ishita around, her laughter echoing through the room like a melody he could never play. It was a sound that filled him with a strange mix of bitterness and longing. It was the sound of happiness, a happiness he felt forever barred from experiencing.

The final note faded away, leaving a heavy silence in its wake. The applause erupted, showering Ishank and Ishita with waves of appreciation. Anesh remained rooted to the spot, a hollow ache settling deep within him.

Psychowrath

He stole a glance at Ishita and Ishank. They were surrounded by a group of friends, their faces flushed with the joy of the dance. Ishita was looking at Ishank, her eyes sparkling with affection. Anesh felt a single tear roll down his cheek, a silent testament to the love he had lost.

He knew he couldn't stay there any longer. Every breath in that room felt like a betrayal, a constant reminder of his own failures. With a heavy heart, he slipped out of the party unnoticed, disappearing into the cool night air.

As Anesh walked home, the weight of his unspoken feelings pressed down on him like a physical burden. He reached a deserted stretch of road, the silence broken only by the rhythmic chirping of crickets in the nearby fields. The town lights twinkled faintly in the distance, a stark contrast to the inky blackness that surrounded him.

Lost in his thoughts, he didn't notice Ishank approach until a hand landed on his shoulder.

"Hey, there you are," Ishank said softly, his voice laced with concern. "Didn't see you slip out. Everything alright?"

Anesh flinched, startled from his reverie. He whirled around to face his best friend, his emotions a roiling tempest within him. For a long moment, he stood there in silence, the unspoken words hanging heavy in the air.

Finally, Anesh blurted out the question that had been consuming him all night, his voice thick with a raw mix of pain and betrayal, "Do you love her?"

Ishank's brow furrowed in confusion. "Love who?" he asked, his voice laced with genuine bewilderment. "What are you talking about, Anesh?"

Anesh took a shaky breath, his throat tight with unshed tears. "Ishita," he choked out, the name a single, desperate word. "Do you love Ishita?"

The question hung in the air, heavy with unspoken accusations. Ishank hesitated, his gaze flickering away from Anesh's intense stare. He ran a hand through his hair, a gesture that betrayed his growing unease.

Letting out a defeated sigh, he spoke, his voice laced with regret, "Look, Anesh, I was just about to tell you. We... we've been seeing each other for a while now. I'm truly sorry I didn't say anything before. I know you're furious, feeling like I, your best friend, kept this huge secret from you, but-"

Anesh cut him off, a single, humorless bark of a laugh escaping his lips. "Seeing each other?" he repeated, the words laced with irony. "Is that what you call it, Ishank? A clandestine affair while I pined away in blissful ignorance?"

Ishank flinched at the harshness in Anesh's voice, a flicker of hurt crossing his features. "It wasn't like that," he defended himself, his voice low and earnest. "We... things just kind of developed between us. It wasn't planned, Anesh, you have to believe me."

Anesh's world crumbled around him, the reality he knew fracturing like a shattered mirror. The anger that had been simmering beneath his skin, a low hum in his veins, suddenly erupted like a violent geyser. Before Ishank could even shape the final words of his apology, Anesh lunged at him, spurred by betrayal, and hurt.

A gruesome struggle unfolded under the cold, aloof gaze of the moon. It was a disturbing dance, an intimate ballet steeped in rage and despair. The details of the struggle morphed into a nightmarish kaleidoscope – the lethal gleam of metal, a gasp cut short by fear, the horrifying sound of a body colliding with the unyielding earth.

"You were my closest ally, Ishank," Anesh spat, his voice laced with venom. "You, of all people, should have recognized my feelings for Ishita." His words hung heavy in the air, a testament of his deep-rooted resentment. "But now, now that you've intruded between her and me, you leave me with no choice but to end your life."

Ishank, groaning in pain, struggled to respond. "What are you doing, Anesh? Have you forgotten our bond?"

Anesh's laughter was harsh and cruel. "What kind of bond allows one to steal another's love? How can I trust such a friend?"

In a feeble attempt to reason, Ishank appealed to his sensibilities. "Don't lose yourself to madness, Anesh. You risk ruining your life. Ishita will never love a beast."

Anesh's only reply was a chilling farewell. "Goodbye, old friend."

With renewed fury, Anesh attacked the prone figure of his once friend. Ishank's consciousness flickered and then extinguished under the brutal assault. Anesh then began the grim task of dragging Ishank, his body lifeless and heavy, towards the edge of a steep precipice that overlooked a dense forest.

The earth under his feet crumbled, mirroring his sanity. Each step he took was a descent into a darker abyss of madness. Upon reaching the precipice, Anesh stared down into the yawning chasm below. The wind tugged at his clothes and hair, a cold caress on his face, carrying with it the chilling cries of unseen creatures lurking in the darkness.

Psychowrath

He heaved Ishank's body over the edge, watching as it disappeared into the inky blackness. He was left alone with the echoes of his actions and the cold indifference of the moon above.

His hands, stained with betrayal and blood, hung heavy at his sides. The wind continued to howl, a mournful hymn to the tragic turn of events. His heart pounded in his chest, a frantic rhythm of regret and satisfaction. As the reality of his actions began to sink in, Anesh's world, once filled with love and friendship, was now a desolate landscape of guilt and solitude.

The moon, his sole witness, cast long shadows that danced grotesquely on the ground. The forest below seemed to swallow his heavy footsteps as he walked away from the precipice. The cries of the night creatures were his only company, a haunting symphony that played the score of his betrayal.

Anesh had descended into a realm where his love for Ishita had turned him into a monster. His hands, once a source of comfort and friendship, were now tools of destruction. His heart, once teeming with love, was now a breeding ground for regret.

Anesh's mind drifted back to when he and Ishank were just boys, inseparable and full of dreams. They had met in the third grade, two shy kids who found solace in each other's company.

Anesh remembered the day they first spoke, during a group project that neither of them wanted to do alone. From that moment on, they were thick as thieves. They did everything together. After school, they would race to the playground, their laughter echoing through the neighborhood as they swung on the monkey bars and played tag. Their bond grew deeper with every shared secret, every sleepover where they stayed up late whispering about their dreams and fears.

When they were twelve, they discovered a hidden path in the woods behind their houses. The path led to a small, secluded pond where they would fish and talk about everything under the sun. It was their special place, a sanctuary where they could escape the world and just be themselves.

Anesh recalled the time he broke his arm falling from a tree. Ishank had been right there, his face pale with worry, as he helped Anesh back home. He had stayed by Anesh's side the entire time, even sleeping on the floor of his room to keep him company. That was the kind of friend Ishank was—loyal, caring, and always there when it mattered.

Anesh stumbled back, his legs turning to jelly. He dry-heaved, bile rising in his throat, the metallic tang of blood staining his senses. He looked down at the empty space where Ishank had been just moments ago, a cold dread settling in his gut. He had committed a monstrous act, a crime that would forever stain his soul.

The days that followed were a whirlwind of frantic activity, a desperate attempt to erase the bloody stain on Anesh's conscience. He threw himself into a frenzy of searching, plastering missing person posters around town with trembling hands. His face, etched with fabricated worry, became a constant presence on local news channels. He spoke of Ishank with a choked voice, painting a picture of a loyal friend, a void that could never be filled.

Ishita felt like a fragile porcelain doll that had been carelessly tossed from a speeding car. The world, once a vibrant tapestry woven with love and laughter, had dissolved into a dull, fragmented mess. A gaping hole had been ripped into her chest, sucking out the very air that sustained her. The warmth that had emanated from Ishank's presence, the echo of his voice, the memory of his touch - all these were now agonizing phantoms that haunted her every waking moment.

Sleep, when it came, offered no solace. It was a battlefield where nightmares raged, replaying Ishank's final moments in gruesome detail. Each morning, she woke with a jolt, the harsh reality slamming into her like a tidal wave, stealing her breath and plunging her back into the suffocating abyss of grief.

The world seemed to move in slow motion around her, muted and distant. Familiar faces blurred into unrecognizable shapes, their voices a dull roar that failed to penetrate the fog of her despair. Even the most basic tasks felt herculean, requiring a monumental effort of will that left her drained and trembling.

A bone-deep loneliness gnawed at her, an emptiness that echoed Ishank's absence. The future, once a canvas painted with dreams and aspirations, stretched before her like a barren wasteland, devoid of color and purpose. All that remained was a suffocating sense of loss, a soul-crushing weight that threatened to drag her under.

Her world crumbling around her, clung to Anesh like a lifeline. Her tear-stained face, the raw vulnerability in her eyes, was a constant reminder of the innocent life Anesh had stolen. But amidst the crushing guilt, a chilling calculation bloomed within him. He saw an opportunity, a twisted path towards redemption, or at least, a semblance of it.

He became Ishita's rock, a pillar of strength in the face of her despair. He listened to her recount cherished memories of Ishank, each word a searing ember on his soul. He comforted her with whispered platitudes, his voice a soothing balm that masked the churning darkness within. He even shed a few well-placed tears, his performance so convincing that even he began to question the line between truth and the elaborate lie he was weaving.

He reveled in their misplaced empathy, the false image a shield against the gnawing guilt that threatened to consume him.

He became the embodiment of the concerned friend, organizing search parties, scouring the woods with a fervor that bordered on the obsessive. All the while, a chilling calmness settled over him, a terrifying realization that he could manipulate emotions, orchestrate a performance so convincing that it blurred the lines between reality and his carefully constructed facade.

However, the charade wasn't without its cracks. The nightmares, vivid and horrifying, plagued his sleep. He'd wake up in a cold sweat, the image of Ishank's accusing eyes seared into his mind. The silence of his room became deafening, the absence of Ishank's booming laughter a constant reminder of his monstrous act. He started at every creak of the floorboard, every rustle of leaves outside his window, a constant state of hypervigilance fueled by the fear of discovery.

Would the truth ever come out? Will Anesh succeed in getting what he wants, or will there be a new obstacle in the journey for him?

Chapter Two: The Last ride

Everything is fair in love and war.

~MR. John Lyly

Only a few weeks remained before the pivotal 12th-grade board examinations, and Anesh and Ishita found themselves immersed in intensive preparation. The absence of Ishank lingered in their minds persistently. Despite this, they committed themselves to their studies, soon finding rhythm in their daily routines. They faced the examinations with resolute determination and unwavering effort.

Months blurred by, culminating in the long-awaited release of their 12th-grade results. The air crackled with nervous energy as students crowded around bulletin boards, hearts pounding in their chests. Anesh and Ishita stood shoulder-to-shoulder, a silent understanding passing between them.

When Anesh saw his results, a wave of relief washed over him. He'd aced them, his name even topping the list as the school valedictorian. This achievement, a culmination of years of dedicated studying, opened doors to some of the country's most prestigious colleges. But the thrill of victory was muted by the uncertainty gnawing at him.

His gaze flickered to Ishita, her face breaking into a wide smile as she scanned her own results. Relief and a hint of excitement shone in her eyes, but where would this excitement take her?

As they discussed their options, Ishita's voice held a yearning for a change of scenery. She craved new experiences, a world beyond the familiar confines of their small town. Her sights landed on a well-respected college in Chandigarh, a vibrant city bustling with life and opportunity. While the college offered a great education, it wasn't quite the academic powerhouse Anesh deserved.

Without hesitation, Anesh made a decision that surprised everyone. He enrolled in the same college as Ishita, prioritizing his desire to be near her over the academic prestige he could have achieved elsewhere. College life was a whirlwind of new experiences for both.

The freedom and independence were exhilarating, and Anesh reveled in seeing Ishita blossom in this new environment. They explored the city together, discovering hidden cafes and bustling markets. He found joy in simply being with her, even if it meant trailing behind her sometimes, a lovesick shadow content with just watching her smile.

The air hung heavy with the scent of old books and brewing anxiety. Ishita chewed on the end of her pen, frustration gnawing at her. Beside her, Anesh scribbled furiously, a crease etched between his brows. They were tackling a particularly gnarly calculus equation, the kind that seemed designed to induce existential dread in unsuspecting engineering students.

Suddenly, a shadow fell across their open textbooks. Anesh looked up, startled, to see a tall, lanky figure leaning over them. The newcomer had a mop of unruly black hair that defied gravity and a smile as warm as the afternoon sun filtering through the library windows.

"Hey, need a hand with that equation?" his voice was friendly, laced with a hint of amusement.

Anesh felt a flicker of irritation rise within him. Here he was, struggling with the damn thing, and this guy waltzed in with an air of effortless confidence.

"Uh, yeah," Anesh stammered, suddenly self-conscious about his messy notes and furrowed brow. "It's got us stumped."

The newcomer grinned, extending a hand. "Sandeep, but everyone calls me Sandy. No worries, equations are my jam."

Ishita, who had been quietly observing the exchange, felt a spark of interest ignite. Sandy's casual confidence was a refreshing change from the tense atmosphere she and Anesh had created around the problem. She watched as he skimmed the equation, his brow furrowing momentarily before a triumphant grin spread across his face.

"Ah, I see the culprit here," he said, tapping a specific point on the page. "This term's a bit tricky, but a simple substitution should do the trick."

With effortless ease, Sandy broke down the equation, explaining each step in a clear, concise manner. He used analogies and visual aids, transforming the complex problem into something almost…fun. Ishita found herself leaning in, her earlier anxiety replaced by a genuine fascination with his approach.

Anesh, on the other hand, couldn't help but feel a pang of insecurity. Here he was, a self-proclaimed math whiz, struggling with the problem, and this newcomer breezed in like a conquering hero.

"There you go," Sandy finished, a playful glint in his eyes. "All solved! Did that make sense?"

Ishita's eyes sparkled with newfound understanding. "Absolutely! Thank you, Sandy, you're a lifesaver."

Anesh mumbled a thanks, his voice strained.

"No problem at all," Sandy replied, his smile genuine. "I'm actually new here. I just transferred this semester. You guys must be…"

"Ishita," she interjected, extending her hand. "And this is Anesh."

Sandy's handshake was firm and warm. "Nice to meet you both. So, what brings you to the wonderful world of calculus?"

"We're both first-year engineering students," she explained. "Trying to navigate the treacherous waters of math's and physics."

Sandy chuckled. "Believe me, I know the feeling. I grew up in a small village back in Punjab. Never thought I'd see the inside of a fancy university library like this one."

His casual mention of his rural background surprised Ishita. There was no self-pity or bitterness in his voice, just a matter-of-fact acceptance. She found herself curious about his journey.

"Wow, that's a big change," she said, surprised. "What made you decide to come here?"

"My father always said education was the key to unlocking possibilities," Sandy replied, a touch of pride in his voice. "He worked incredibly hard to give me the best education he could afford. Even though resources were limited back home, I managed to score well in my 12th grade exams. This scholarship opportunity fell into my lap, and I grabbed it with both hands."

Psychowrath

Ishita felt a wave of respect wash over her. Sandy's journey resonated with her. He wasn't just some effortlessly brilliant guy; he was someone who had worked hard and overcome challenges to get where he was.

From the moment he arrived on campus, Sandy's kindness and helpfulness earned him a reputation as a beacon of sunshine. He quickly became a part of their group, his easy-going nature and quick wit adding a new dimension to their friendship.

Anesh felt a pang of something akin to jealousy when Ishita's eyes lit up with Sandy's arrival. He watched, a knot forming in his stomach, as they delved into a discussion about complex calculus problems, their laughter echoing through the library. Anesh, who had always been Ishita's confidante and study partner, felt a strange sense of exclusion. He realized, with a jolt, that their dynamic was changing, and a seed of uncertainty began to sprout within him.

As time flowed, the bond between Ishita and Sandy blossomed. He often gave her rides back to their apartment complex on his motorbike, a sight that filled Anesh with a cold dread one afternoon. The casual way Ishita perched on the back of Sandy's bike, her laughter echoing in the air, sent a jolt of jealousy through him. A primal urge to possess Ishita, to chase away this newfound rival, bubbled up within him. But blind rage wouldn't solve anything. He needed a plan.

Then, fate, or perhaps something more sinister lurking within Anesh, intervened. He discovered that Sandy had a younger sister, Ruhi. Unlike Ishita, who thrived in academics, Ruhi was an artist, her soul yearning for self-expression through vibrant strokes and bold colors. While her academic performance was less than stellar, her talent was undeniable – she'd bagged several prestigious art awards at the state and national level.

Up until now, their interactions had been minimal, polite hellos exchanged in passing. But Anesh, ever the strategist, saw an opportunity in Ruhi.

By that time, Anesh had managed to wrangle a decent income through various freelance gigs. He decided to exploit this newfound financial independence. Feigning a newfound interest in art, he showered Ruhi with compliments on her work and offered to help her with the academic subjects she found challenging.

Ruhi, initially wary of this sudden attention, found herself warming up to Anesh's easygoing charm and genuine-seeming interest in her art. His 'gifts' weren't limited to academic pointers; he started presenting her with high-quality art supplies, further fueling her creative passion.

Ruhi, young and naive, couldn't help but be drawn to Anesh's attentiveness. A subtle, predatory smile played on his lips – his plan, it seemed, was working flawlessly. But his interest in art was a carefully constructed facade. What he truly craved was information. Details about Ruhi, her family, and most importantly, Sandy. He subtly steered their conversations, inquiring about Sandy's daily routine, his hobbies, his likes and dislikes. Ruhi, excited to share her world with someone who seemed genuinely interested, spilled the beans, unknowingly becoming a pawn in Anesh's intricate game.

Days blurred together, each one a monotonous tick towards the twisted revenge Anesh craved. Ruhi, unknowingly a pawn in his elaborate game, had provided him with a crucial piece of information – a casual tidbit about Sandy's supposed weekend solitude at his family's farm. It was the perfect opportunity, Anesh thought, a chance to confront Sandy and somehow diminish his growing connection with Ishita. His mind, consumed by a dangerous obsession, meticulously crafted a plan, transforming him from a friend into a predator stalking its prey.

The first night arrived, cloaked in an unnatural stillness. Nervous anticipation clawed at Anesh as he crept towards the farmhouse, his heart a frantic drum against his ribs. He reached the edge of the property, his breath fogging in the cool night air. Peeking through a gap in the fence, his vision blurred with a crushing disappointment. There, bathed in the soft glow of the moon, sat Sandy, not alone as Anesh had hoped, but with a figure he presumed to be his father. They were deep in conversation, their faces etched with a quiet understanding.

Disheartened and frustrated, Anesh retreated into the shadows. The week that followed was an agonizing slog. Every stolen glance at Ishita and Sandy laughing together ignited a fresh wave of animosity within him. His once-friendly eyes burned with a hatred that threatened to consume him, a monstrous reflection of the darkness festering in his soul.

Meanwhile, oblivious to the storm brewing within Anesh, Ruhi's affection for him blossomed. She decided to take a chance, her heart pounding with a nervous hope. A message flickered on Anesh's phone, a fluttering invitation to meet on Sunday – a silent plea for something more than their newfound friendship.

The following Saturday night had barely begun to relinquish its hold in the sky when Anesh, fueled by a stubborn flicker of hope that he couldn't quite explain, found himself back at the farmhouse.

The days since his initial failed attempt had been a rollercoaster of despair and a strange, desperate courage. He tiptoed through the tall corn stalks, the only sound of the dry leaves crunching ominously under his feet. He reached the open field, and his breath hitched in his throat. There, under the dim moonlight, sprawled on a blanket in the middle of the field, lay Sandy. Anesh's heart pounded a frantic rhythm against his ribs – this time, he thought with a chilling certainty, nothing would stand in his way.

The inky cloak of night had settled over the town, swallowing the vibrant hues of day and replacing them with an unsettling darkness. Anesh, a shadow against the shadows, moved with a practiced ease towards the field where Sandy laid untroubled. The only sounds were the rhythmic creak of the crickets and the distant howl of a lone coyote. An unsettling calm draped over him, a mask for the storm brewing within. He picked up a spade, the weight a grim comfort in his hand. As he drew closer, a practiced ease veiled his movements, lulling Sandy into a false sense of security.

Then, with a cold-blooded swiftness that sent a shiver down his own spine, Anesh struck. The clang of metal on bone echoed through the empty field, a sickening counterpoint to the chirping crickets. Sandy crumpled, a strangled cry escaping his lips as blood welled from a horrific gash on his face. Through the haze, he saw Anesh's face contorted in a mask of rage, a glint of manic glee in his eyes. Anesh felt a surge of dark satisfaction, a twisted validation.

"Anesh... what is this?" Sandy rasped, clutching his throbbing face. His voice came out choked and disoriented. "Why...?"

A chilling laugh escaped Anesh's lips, devoid of any humor. "Don't play dumb, Sandy. You think I haven't seen the way you look at Ishita? The way she smiles at you? It's all a game to you, isn't it?"

Sandy's confusion deepened, the pain in his face a dull throb compared to the bewilderment twisting his gut. "Ishita... what are you talking about? We're just friends, Anesh. Friends!"

His words seemed to ignite Anesh's fury further. "Friends? Don't lie to me! I see the way she leans in when you talk, the way her eyes light up. You're after her, just like everyone else."

Anesh's voice dripped with paranoia; his words laced with a bitterness that sent a shiver down Sandy's spine.

"Anesh, listen to me," Sandy pleaded, his voice laced with a tremor of fear. "There's nothing going on between me and Ishita."

But Anesh was lost in his own delusional world. "Don't try to weasel your way out of this," he snarled, advancing towards Sandy with a predatory glint in his eyes.

But a primal growl shattered his intentions. Tyson, Sandy's loyal Doberman, emerged from behind a hay bale, fangs bared, a low rumble vibrating in his throat.

Anesh, caught off guard, felt a searing pain as the dog sank its teeth into his hand. Panic flared, momentarily eclipsing the cold calculation. He whipped out his pocketknife, the glint of metal a chilling contrast to the sliver of moon peeking through the clouds. The struggle was brief, fueled by primal fear on both sides. An agonizing yelp, choked off abruptly, marked the end of the fight. Tyson lay still, a silent guardian forever silenced.

Anesh turned back to Sandy, who had dragged himself towards his bike, a pathetic attempt at escape. Blood painted a grotesque masterpiece on his clothes, his face a mask of terror illuminated by the pale moonlight.

"What did you think, huh?" Anesh's voice was a low growl, laced with a terrible glee. "Ishika? Did you think a few sweet words would win her over? I've known her for years, watched her from the sidelines like a lovesick fool. And you waltz in and think you can just have her?"

With practiced efficiency, he bound Sandy's wrists and ankles, then secured him to the motorcycle alongside Tyson's lifeless body. A cold smile played on his lips as he doused them both in gasoline, the metallic tang a final, grotesque detail.

A single spark from his lighter ignited the inferno. Sandy's scream, a horrifying chorus of pain and despair, was swallowed by the roar of the flames. Anesh watched, detached, as the fire consumed everything, leaving behind only a smoldering pyre and the acrid stench of death.

He walked away, a solitary figure swallowed by the darkness, leaving no trace except for the ashes of his crimes and a chilling secret burning in his heart.

Sunday dawned, a fragile promise of normalcy. Ruhi, a kaleidoscope of butterflies in her stomach, prepared to meet Anesh at their usual cafe. Today, she planned to confess the burgeoning feelings that had taken root in her heart. But as Anesh arrived, a discordant note shattered the hopeful melody. His hand, usually bare, was now obscured by a clumsy bandage.

"What happened?" Ruhi asked, furrowing her brow.

Anesh chuckled; a touch too forced. "Nothing serious," he said, waving his hand dismissively. "Just a spill from the bike yesterday."

Ruhi's brow furrowed further. "You don't own a bike, do you?"

Anesh hesitated. "Well, actually," he stammered, "it was one I borrowed."

A sliver of unease wormed its way into Ruhi's gut. Then, as Anesh settled into his chair, she noticed a telltale smudge on his shoe – a clump of dirt identical to the one found in the secluded field she frequented. Ignoring the tremor of suspicion, she pushed on, determined to share her feelings.

"Anesh," she began, her voice trembling slightly, "there's something I need to tell you."

Anesh's smile faltered, a flicker of concern crossing his face. "What is it, Ruhi? Tell me."

The moment was shattered by the shrill ring of her phone. It was her father. A jolt of apprehension coursed through her. Why would he call me now?

Ruhi answered, her heart pounding a frantic rhythm against her ribs. The conversation that followed was a blur of choked sobs and horrified whispers. The phone slipped from her numb fingers, clattering to the floor.

"Ruhi? What's wrong?" Anesh asked, his voice laced with a fake concern.

But Ruhi was already a blur of movement, fleeing the cafe and the unspoken words that hung heavy in the air. Reaching home, she found it a house of mourning. Faces etched with grief swam around her.

Her mother, eyes red-rimmed and tear-streaked, wrapped her in a crushing embrace.

"A villager found a body..." her mother's voice hitched, "in our field, with Sandy's bike."

Ruhi's breath hitched. Sandy, her brother, her confidante, her pillar of strength – gone? The world seemed to tilt on its axis. She clung to her mother; a silent scream trapped in her throat.

The news spread like wildfire through the close-knit community. The discovery – a charred frame of a motorcycle, a pile of smoldering ashes – painted a grim picture.

The police arrived; their faces grim as they surveyed the scene. Samples were taken, whispers of "accidents" and "tragic mishaps" filling the air.

Days bled into weeks. The official report, a cold, clinical document, confirmed the ashes belonged to Sandy. His family, already burdened by the loss of their only son, reeled under the weight of a grief deemed accidental. Ruhi, caught between her love for her family and the nagging suspicion that gnawed at her, felt increasingly isolated.

Her parents, consumed by their sorrow, withdrew into a shell of their former selves. Conversations became strained, smiles a distant memory.

Psychowrath

Ruhi knew something was off, she was not ready to accept the fact that it was an accident.

Anesh, numb to the horror, found a perverse satisfaction in his actions. Was this love, or a descent into madness?

Chapter Three: Game of Thorns

Love is a game of thorns. Play at your own risk.

~Author

The first year of college had flown by in a whirlwind of lectures, late-night study sessions, and the nervous thrill of newfound independence. Now, as summer break ended, students trickled back onto campus, buzzing anticipating the new semester. Among them was Anesh, his heart pounding a frantic rhythm against his ribs.

In the first year, the classes of Anesh and Ishita were different. That's why, this year held a particular significance – he'd be sharing his classes with Ishita.

The news had filled him with a giddy euphoria. Their bond, once strong, had frayed over the last one year. He yearned to bridge the gap, to rekindle the spark that had ignited in their first year. Fate, it seemed, was on his side. A class reshuffle placed them side-by-side, offering Anesh the perfect opportunity to reinsert himself into her life.

Their friendship wasn't destined to blossom in a quiet, one-on-one setting. This year, they'd be joined by Samaira, a whirlwind of energy and infectious laughter. She was the life of the party, the one who could turn a dull Tuesday into a spontaneous adventure. Ishita, naturally drawn to Samaira's vibrancy, had become her closest friend, sharing a cramped but cozy apartment and confiding secrets whispered late at night.

Anesh, initially daunted by Samaira's presence, quickly realized she was a bridge, not a barrier. Together, the three became inseparable, a chaotic trio dubbed "The Chunks" by their classmates. They filled their days with laughter, dissecting everything from the latest campus gossip to the meaning of life during long lunches in the canteen. Whether huddled in a corner of the library or sprawled on the grass under a star-dusted sky, they were a haven for each other, a refuge from the pressures of college life.

Anesh meticulously cultivated a charming facade, playing the perfect friend while harboring a secret yearning. He was confident, almost arrogant, in his belief that Ishita would eventually reciprocate his feelings.

As the semester ended, the annual college festival loomed on the horizon, a vibrant celebration pulsating with music and revelry. For Anesh, it was more than just a festival; it was a stage, a platform for his grand romantic gesture, the culmination of a year of silent planning.

However, Samaira, ever the chatterbox, was about to unwittingly drop a bombshell that would throw a wrench into Anesh's carefully constructed plan. A single sentence, tossed out with the casualness of discussing the weather, would set in motion a chain of events that would shatter the comfortable bubble of The Chunks.

One afternoon, as Ishita and Samaira were sprawled on Ishita's bed, flipping through a magazine, Samaira fidgeted nervously, a blush creeping up her neck.

Ishita, noticing her friend's unease, nudged her playfully. "Sam, what's got you all flustered? Spill the beans!"

Samaira gnawed on her lip, her voice barely a whisper. "There's something I need to tell you, Ishita. I've been holding onto it for weeks, but I just can't keep it bottled up any longer."

Intrigued, Ishita scooted closer, her eyes wide with concern. "Whoa, that sounds serious! Did something happen? Did you fight with your parents again?"

Samaira shook her head, a shy smile gracing her lips. "Not exactly. It's more like... there's someone I have feelings for, and it's been weighing heavily on my heart."

Ishita's eyebrows shot up. "Wait, really? You found someone special? Come on, don't leave me hanging! Tell me all about this mystery crush!"

Taking a deep breath, Samaira blurted out, "It's... well, it's Anesh."

"Anesh!" she exclaimed, a wide grin replacing her initial surprise. "That's amazing, Samaira! You lucky duck! He's such a great guy, genuine and funny. You have a good eye. I'm sure he feels the same way, and I'm absolutely thrilled for you both!"

Samaira's face lit up, a radiant smile chasing away the earlier nervousness. Relief washed over her as she gushed about the little moments with Anesh that had made her heart skip a beat – his infectious laughter, his willingness to help her with a particularly tricky math problem.

As the conversation flowed, they made plans to set Anesh and Samaira up, to nudge them together and see where things went. The upcoming festival, a vibrant celebration of music, dance, and delicious food, seemed like the perfect opportunity. They pictured Anesh, caught off guard by Samaira's radiant beauty, and Samaira, finally finding the courage to confess her feelings. It would be a night to remember, a night that could blossom into something beautiful.

The festival buzzed with anticipation as The Chunks gathered for their annual outing. The air thrummed with music, a vibrant tapestry of sound woven from lively folk tunes and energetic dance beats. The scent of sizzling kebabs and sweet, sugary treats mingled in the air, a tantalizing invitation to indulge. Strings of colorful lights cast a warm glow on the bustling crowd, creating a magical atmosphere.

Ishita, ever the fashionista, was a vision in a sapphire maxi dress. The flowing fabric skimmed her figure gracefully, its deep blue hue echoing the twilight sky. Delicate straps offered a touch of sophistication, while sparkling chandelier earrings added a hint of glamor. She had kept her makeup minimal, allowing her natural beauty to shine through. With a confident smile that could light up the night, Ishita was ready to conquer the festival.

Not to be outdone, Samaira embodied a fiery spirit in a dress that matched. The bold red color clung to her curves in all the right places, turning heads as she moved with a newfound confidence. A single statement necklace completed the look, adding a touch of elegance to her bold choice. A glint of determination sparkled in her eyes, hinting at the special significance of this night for her.

Anesh, however, felt a knot of nervousness tighten in his stomach as he scanned the throng of people. His carefully chosen outfit – a crisp white button-down paired with dark slacks – suddenly fell out of place amidst the dazzling dresses and festive atmosphere. He took a deep breath, smoothing down his suddenly rumpled tie, his resolve hardening with each passing moment.

Anesh stole glances at Ishita, his heart fluttering like a trapped bird in his chest. Her beauty tonight was undeniable, bathed in the warm glow of the festival lights. It was the night he'd planned to finally gather the courage to confess his feelings, but with every stolen glance, his carefully rehearsed words seemed to vanish into thin air. He fidgeted with his tie, a silent reassurance in the face of his growing nervousness.

Ishita, noticing Samaira's flushed cheeks and shy smile as she chatted with a group of friends, couldn't help but grin. Turning to Anesh, she said, "Wow, Anesh, you look sharp tonight." Great outfit!"

His surprise at the unexpected compliment was evident. A warmth bloomed in his chest, chasing away some of his nervous tension. "Thanks, Ishita," he stammered, much more confident than before.

He desperately wanted to return the compliment, to find the perfect words to describe the way Ishita's sapphire dress hugged her curves and shimmered under the fairy lights. But the fear of sounding cheesy or overly familiar held him back. Instead, he blurted out, "Uh, you look... really nice too."

Ishita chuckled, the sound like wind chimes in the summer breeze. "Creative, Anesh," she teased, her eyes sparkling with amusement. "But I appreciate it.

Though, in that case, maybe you should save your compliments for Samaira. She's practically glowing tonight!"

Samaira, who had caught the tail end of their conversation, blushed a deep crimson. "Oh, stop it, you guys!" she protested playfully. "Let's just enjoy the festival, shall we? Otherwise, the night will fly by in a blur of compliments."

As the vibrant sounds of music and laughter filled the air, Anesh found himself drawn into conversations with various friends. Yet, his gaze kept returning to Ishita, watching her dance with carefree abandon, her smile infectious. He yearned to join her, to lose himself in the rhythm of the music with her, but the fear of rejection kept him rooted to the spot.

The night progressed, the vibrant energy of the festival slowly giving way to a more relaxed atmosphere. As the last strains of music faded, and the food stalls began to close for the night, Anesh knew his moment had arrived. He needed to talk to Ishita, to confess his true feelings.

Anesh fidgeted with his phone, the minutes stretching into an eternity. He kept glancing at the entrance, his heart hammering a frantic rhythm against his ribs. Where was Ishita?

He desperately needed to talk to her, to confess the darkness that clouded his conscience and, more importantly, to express the feelings he'd kept bottled up for far too long.

Suddenly, a familiar voice broke the tension. Samaira stood before him, her cheeks flushed a delicate pink, her eyes shimmering with a mix of nervousness and determination. "Anesh," she began, her voice barely above a whisper, "There's something I've been wanting to tell you for a while now. And I think it's finally time I get it off my chest."

Anesh felt a jolt of surprise course through him. He hadn't anticipated this turn of events. "Sure, Samaira," he stammered, his voice betraying his surprise. "What is it?"

Taking a deep breath, Samaira blurted out, "The truth is, Anesh, I... I have feelings for you. It's been there for a while now, but I just couldn't bring myself to say anything. But tonight, I felt like I had to take a chance."

An honest confession hung heavy in the air. An unexpected twist in the carefully constructed plan that had been churning in his mind. A wave of guilt washed over him, a bitter aftertaste for the darkness he'd almost unleashed. He cared for Samaira, truly. She was a kind and funny friend, a constant source of

support and laughter. But the feelings she harbored –
those were reserved for someone else entirely.

"Samaira," he began, his voice laced with sincerity, "I
appreciate you being so honest with me. It means a
lot. But the truth is, I don't have those feelings for
you in the same way. We've always been great friends,
and I value that friendship a lot. I hope you
understand."

Disappointment clouded Samaira's eyes, a silent tear
threatening to spill over. "I... I see," she stammered,
her voice trembling slightly. "Maybe I was wrong.
Excuse me for a moment, I just need some air."

With a choked sob, Samaira turned and hurried away,
disappearing into the throng of people. Anesh stole a
glance around, searching for Ishita, hoping she hadn't
witnessed the exchange.

As if sensing his gaze, Ishita materialized beside him,
her brow furrowed with concern. "What happened,
Anesh? Why did Samaira run off?"

Anesh released a shaky breath, the weight of his
unspoken confession pressing down on him. He had
to get the words out, to finally tell Ishita the truth
about his feelings.

"Ishita, Samaira just confessed her feelings for me,"
he began, his voice barely a whisper. "But the truth is,
I don't feel the same way about her. It's you, Ishita.

I've had feelings for you for a long time now. Tonight felt like the right moment to tell you."

He took a deep breath, his heart pounding a frantic rhythm against his ribs. "There's so much I love about you, Ishita. Your eyes, the way they sparkle with laughter and kindness. Your voice, it's like a melody that fills me with warmth. You're beautiful, Ishita, inside and out."

The words tumbled out; a torrent of emotions he'd held bottled up for too long. He watched Ishita's face, searching for a flicker of recognition, a hint of reciprocation. But her expression remained unreadable, a mix of surprise and something deeper he couldn't quite decipher.

"Anesh," she said softly, her voice laced with concern, "This is all so unexpected. We've been friends since our school days, practically inseparable. I never thought of you in a romantic way."

A shard of disappointment pierced his heart. He had built his hopes up, convinced that his feelings were mirrored in hers. The years of shared laughter, whispered secrets, and unspoken bonds – had they all just been a figment of his imagination?

"We are just friends, Anesh," Ishita continued, her voice gentle but firm. "And I value that friendship a lot. I appreciate your honesty, but I don't want to complicate things. Even if I lied and said I felt the same way, it wouldn't be true. And that wouldn't be fair to you, or to Samaira."

Her words were kind, but they felt like a rejection all the same. A cold dread settled in his stomach, the weight of his confession crushing him. He understood her perspective, the sanctity of their friendship, but the pain of her rejection was sharp and undeniable.

An overwhelming sense of dejection washed over him. The past few years, the sacrifices he'd made, the darkness he'd almost succumbed to – it all felt pointless now. He had done it all for her, or so he thought. Now, he was left questioning everything.

Silence descended between them, thick and heavy. Anesh couldn't meet Ishita's gaze, the sting of rejection burning in his eyes. He felt like a fool, his grand confession reduced to a mere footnote in their friendship.

Ishita, sensing his despair, placed a comforting hand on his arm. "Anesh," she said softly, "I know this hurts. But trust me, honesty is always the best policy. Samaira is a wonderful person, kind and beautiful. Maybe you should take some time to think about her feelings? You never know what the future holds."

Ishita's heart ached for her friend. Seeing Samaira huddled by the pool, tears staining her cheeks, ignited a wave of protectiveness within her. She approached cautiously, unsure of how to offer comfort.

"Hey, Samaira," Ishita said softly, her voice laced with concern. "Is everything alright?"

Samaira barely acknowledged her presence, her shoulders shaking with silent sobs. "It's nothing, Ishita," she mumbled, wiping furiously at her eyes. "Just leave me alone, please."

Ishita hesitated, torn between giving Samaira space and offering a listening ear. A flicker of annoyance sparked within her, quickly extinguished by a deeper well of empathy. "Okay, Samaira," she conceded gently. "Take your time. But know that I'm here for you if you want to talk."

With a heavy heart, Ishita walked away, leaving Samaira alone with her grief. As she disappeared into the throng of people, a dark figure emerged from the shadows. Anesh, his face obscured by the night, stalked towards the sobbing girl, his movements silent and menacing. Samaira, lost in her despair, remained oblivious to the approaching danger.

"Samaira," Anesh's voice was a low murmur, sending a shiver down her spine. She looked up with startled eyes, a flicker of hope igniting in their depths.

"Anesh?" Her voice trembled, barely a whisper.

"I wanted to apologize," he said, his voice smooth as butter, a stark contrast to the coldness in his eyes. "I acted impulsively earlier. Perhaps I..." He trailed off, letting the silence hang heavy in the air, his words carefully chosen to manipulate her emotions.

Samaira's heart hammered against her ribs. Could this be her chance? A sliver of hope, fragile yet persistent, bloomed in her chest. "Perhaps you...?" she prompted, her voice barely audible.

A cruel smile played on Anesh's lips, hidden from Samaira's view by the darkness. "Perhaps I've realized my feelings for you, Samaira," he finished, his voice dripping with false sincerity.

Tears welled up in Samaira's eyes once more, this time tears of joy. Relief washed over her, chasing away the remnants of her earlier heartbreak. Before she could respond, Anesh lunged forward, his hand shooting out like a viper's strike. A steely grip clamped around her throat, cutting off her air.

A choked gasp escaped Samaira's lips as she was shoved backwards. The world tilted on its axis as she slammed against the cold stone edge of the pool. Water rushed up to meet her, a suffocating embrace. Panic surged through her veins, clawing at her throat. She clawed desperately at Anesh's hand, her pleas for mercy turning into silent bubbles escaping through her lips.

But Anesh remained a cold, unfeeling statue. He watched with a detached coldness as the light faded from Samaira's eyes, the life slowly draining from her body. Her final struggle, a desperate thrash against the inevitable, was a mere ripple in the still water. With a final, gurgling breath, Samaira went limp.

Anesh wasted no time. He released his grip, his touch as fleeting as his apology. He vanished into the night like a phantom, leaving no trace behind except for the lifeless body floating in the pool. The music continued to blare, oblivious to the tragedy that had unfolded under the cloak of darkness. The night, once vibrant and alive, now held a sinister secret, a chilling truth waiting to be unearthed.

The first rays of dawn painted the sky a hopeful orange, a stark contrast to the chilling scene that unfolded by the pool. A bloodcurdling scream shattered the peaceful morning, followed by frantic shouts and panicked scrambling. Samaira's lifeless body lay sprawled in the water, a once vibrant flower now wilted and broken.

The wail of sirens sliced through the air, growing louder with each passing second. Soon, the local police swarmed the festival grounds, their faces grim and determined. Inspector Kapoor, a seasoned officer with eyes that held the weight of countless investigations, took charge. The festive atmosphere that had lingered just hours ago was replaced by a chilling efficiency as the officers cordoned off the area.

The investigation began swiftly but hit an immediate snag. There were no obvious signs of struggle, no forced entry, no weapon in sight. The only clue, if it could be called one, was Samaira's distraught state the previous night, as witnessed by Ishita.

Ishita, eyes red-rimmed and voice trembling, recounted the events of the festival. Her heart ached as she spoke of seeing Samaira, her usually bubbly friend, withdrawn and tearful after her rejection by Anesh. The memory brought a fresh wave of grief crashing down on Ishita. Believing Samaira's death a tragic accident, she poured her heart out, unaware of the monstrous secret that lay hidden beneath the surface.

Anesh, too, was brought in for questioning. He played his part flawlessly, his face etched with a convincing mask of grief. Inspector Kapoor studied him intently, his sharp eyes searching for any flicker of guilt or deceit. Anesh, however, held his composure.

"Mr. Kapoor," Anesh began, his voice thick with emotion, "I can't believe Samaira is gone. She was a wonderful person, a true friend. Seeing her so upset last night..." he trailed off, his voice choked by a sob.

He wiped a tear from his eye, the picture of a heartbroken friend.

Inspector Kapoor pressed on; his questions carefully worded. "Did you see anyone else with Samaira last night? Anyone who might have caused her harm?"

Anesh shook his head, his voice barely a whisper. "No, Inspector. I left her by the pool, quite distraught. I had no idea..." He let the sentence hang unfinished, his grief appearing genuine.

The inspector studied him for a long moment, searching for any telltale sign, any crack in the facade. But Anesh remained unfazed. He answered every question with a believable mix of sorrow and confusion. The lack of physical evidence coupled with Anesh's convincing performance left the police with little to go on.

"It appears to be a case of suicide, Inspector," one of the officers chimed in, his voice heavy with regret. The inspector nodded slowly, the weight of the unsolved case settling on his shoulders. The scene mirrored countless others he'd witnessed - a young life tragically cut short, the cause shrouded in a veil of uncertainty.

As the investigation ended, Inspector Kapoor couldn't shake the feeling that something wasn't right. There was a nagging suspicion in his gut, a whisper that something more sinister lay beneath the surface of this apparent suicide. He couldn't put his finger on it, but Anesh's demeanor, a slight shift in his eyes during questioning, left a disquieting feeling. Yet, with no concrete evidence, his hands were tied.

Ishita, meanwhile, was drowning in a sea of grief. The loss of her friend left a gaping hole in her life. The image of Samaira's lifeless body haunted her dreams, a constant reminder of the tragedy.

Chapter Four: Happily Ever After

Life, love and happiness. I want to experience it all with you.

~Anonymous

The absence of Samaira was a constant ache in Ishita's chest. Not a single day passed where the echo of her laughter, the warmth of their shared secrets, didn't flicker through Ishita's mind. Hours would melt away as she reminisced about their bond, the way Samaira could banish even the darkest of moods with her infectious smile, the unwavering support she offered during Ishita's own struggles.

But a nagging doubt gnawed at Ishita's resolve. Sure, Samaira had been devastated by the rejection, but suicide? It just didn't seem right. Samaira wasn't the kind to crumble under a broken heart. She was strong, perceptive – able to read people and situations with a wisdom that defied her young age. Each memory of Samaira chipped away at the fragile foundation Ishita had built in the aftermath of Ishank's passing, Sandy's accident, and now this. A suffocating guilt bloomed in her chest, a noxious vine wrapping itself around her heart. Was it something she'd said, a clue she'd missed? Self-blame became a relentless companion, driving a wedge between her and the world around her.

Ishita retreated further into herself, a shell of the vibrant girl she once was. The sparkle in her eyes, once bright and engaging, dimmed, replaced by a hollow ache that mirrored the emptiness echoing within the walls of her once laughter-filled apartment. The silence was deafening, punctuated only by the rhythmic tick of the clock, a constant reminder of time's relentless march forward while Ishita remained frozen in a sea of grief.

The world outside continued to spin, oblivious to the storm raging within her. Friends called, messages piled up on her phone, but Ishita couldn't bring herself to respond. The effort to interact, of pretending a normalcy that felt a million miles away, was simply too much. Her days blurred into a monotonous routine of aimless movement – getting out of bed, going through the motions of showering and eating, then collapsing back onto the bed, the weight of grief a suffocating blanket.

Sleep, when it came, offered no solace. Dreams became a battlefield of fragmented memories – arguments with Samaira, laughter shared, unanswered calls. She'd wake up in a cold sweat, the sheets tangled around her, the phantom echo of Samaira's voice a cruel taunt in the stillness of the night.

The world outside seemed to lose its vibrancy. Colors dull, sounds muffled, joy a faded memory. Even simple activities, like making a cup of coffee, felt like an insurmountable task. The once familiar routine now seemed daunting, a stark reminder of a life that felt increasingly distant.

Her reflection in the mirror was a stranger – sunken eyes rimmed with red, hair limp and lifeless. The vibrancy that once shone through her smile was extinguished, replaced by a hollow emptiness. The girl who used to face challenges with a determined glint in her eye was gone, replaced by a ghost of her former self.

The guilt was the worst. It gnawed at her relentlessly, a constant whisper in her ear, replaying every conversation, every interaction with Samaira. Had she missed something? Had she not been there for her friend in her darkest hour? These questions became her tormentors, a relentless loop playing on repeat in her mind.

It was time for Anesh's entry now. He knew that there was no one left between him and Ishita, and she was going through the darkest phase of her life.

Reaching out to Ishita was like casting a line into a still pond. Her responses were slow, hesitant, lost in the depths of her own sorrow. But Anesh persisted, his messages a constant, gentle nudge towards the surface. He knew their shared history with The Chunks, their group, could be the key. So, he meticulously chose The Corner Cup, their former hangout, as the battleground for his manipulation.

When Ishita finally arrived, she was a ghost of her former self. The carefree spark in her eyes had been extinguished, replaced by a dull ache and dark circles that spoke of sleepless nights. An ache, unfamiliar and unwelcome, flickered in Anesh's gut. It was a pang of something akin to sympathy, a fleeting emotion he quickly pushed down. This wasn't about sentiment; this was about strategy.

"Ishita," he said, his voice softer than it had been in weeks. "Come, sit."

She shuffled towards the booth; her movements devoid of their usual animation. As they settled in, a heavy silence hung between them, thick with unspoken emotions. Anesh cleared his throat, the sound echoing in the strained atmosphere.

"I know you haven't been back to college since..." he trailed off, his voice carefully neutral, unable to bring himself to utter Samaira's name just yet. "It's been hitting us all hard, you know. Samaira was a friend to me too."

A flicker of surprise, perhaps even a touch of guilt, crossed Ishita's face. "No, Anesh," she whispered, her voice hoarse. "It's all my fault. Everything feels predetermined, like it's written somewhere. First

Ishank, then Sandy, and now Samaira... It's a curse, following me around."

Anesh reached out, his hand hovering cautiously over hers. "Don't say that, Ishita. What happened... it wasn't your fault. They were friends to me as well, and I'm not blaming myself, am I?"

She flinched at his touch, pulling her hand away like a startled bird. "But you're different, Anesh. You..."

"We all grieve, Ishita," he pressed gently, his voice the soothing balm he knew she craved. "Life throws curveballs, things don't always go according to plan. There will be moments of despair, of feeling utterly lost. But we must pick ourselves up, dust ourselves off, and keep going. I want my friend back, Ishita. The strong, vibrant Ishita I know."

A flicker of defiance, a spark of the old Ishita, ignited in her eyes. "You're right, I suppose. I've been wallowing in self-pity for too long. Maybe going back to college would be a good idea. A distraction."

Anesh's smile was a touch too eager, but in Ishita's clouded mind, it went unnoticed. "Exactly!" he exclaimed, a hint of triumph in his voice. "But first things first – dinner with me."

The following days were a carefully orchestrated dance for Anesh. He became Ishita's confidante, a patient listener as she poured out her grief. He offered seemingly harmless advice, encouraging her to reconnect with their old friends, to find solace in routine. Slowly, almost imperceptibly, he began to weave himself into the fabric of her life.

He picked her up for classes, offering a shoulder to lean on as they navigated the crowded hallways. He'd bring her coffee, her favorite kind, a small gesture that felt loaded with meaning.

One fine afternoon, Anesh suggested they grab dinner tonight. Ishita hesitated, then offered a small, hesitant smile. 'Maybe another time,' she replied softly. 'I'm not really in the mood for socializing right now.'"

"Not in the mood for what?" Anesh pressed, his voice losing its usual gentle charm. "Think of it as a way to relax, to take a break from everything. We both need it, wouldn't you agree?"

Anesh steered Ishita away from the harsh glare of the city towards a hidden gem nestled amongst rolling hills. The restaurant was a haven of tranquility, a stark contrast to the turmoil Ishita felt within. Strings of fairy lights cast a warm, intimate glow, chasing away the shadows and creating a tapestry of soft illumination. The air hung heavy with the sweet, inviting aroma of woodsmoke and simmering spices, a promise of delicious meals to come.

Psychowrath

Gentle music, like the murmur of a calming stream, drifted through the open-air space. Unlike the city's relentless cacophony, here, silence reigned supreme, broken only by the soft murmur of conversation and the clinking of silverware. It felt like a world away, a sanctuary where Ishita could shed the weight of her worries, if only for a night. Anesh had chosen well. This oasis of peace might be just the balm she needed, even if his intentions were far from pure.

"Anesh, this place is incredible!" Ishita exclaimed, her voice filled with genuine wonder. "How did I not know about this hidden gem?"

Anesh smiled, a hint of satisfaction playing on his lips. "Perhaps it was meant to be experienced on a special night like this."

A delicate blush crept up Ishita's cheeks. "I never thought you had such a romantic side," she admitted, surprised. "This isn't the kind of place I'd expect you to enjoy."

Anesh chuckled. "Let's just say my stomach was starting to mutiny," he teased. "Besides, exploring new experiences can be rewarding."

Ishita laughed, a light, carefree sound that warmed Anesh's heart. "Good point," she conceded. "Maybe we should ask the waiter for recommendations?"

Anesh readily agreed, and soon they were devouring plates of delicious food, the flavors exploding on their taste buds. Ishita couldn't help but compliment the chef, her eyes sparkling with delight. Watching her animatedly describe each bite, a deep sense of contentment washed over Anesh.

As their meal ended, Anesh excused himself and approached the restaurant manager. A brief conversation ensued, followed by a knowing nod from the manager. A few moments later, a beautifully decorated cake arrived, its surface inscribed with a single, heartfelt message: "I love you so much, Ishita."

Ishita's eyes widened in surprise as she carefully unwrapped the cake. The air crackled with unspoken emotions, a sweet anticipation hanging heavy between them. Anesh watched her, his cheeks flushed a light pink.

"Ishita," he began, his voice thick with emotion, "I know neither of us is going through the easiest time right now. But…" he hesitated, taking a deep breath. "I want things to change. I know I messed up before, but I'm asking you again, Ishita. I care about you deeply. Do you feel the same way?"

His gaze held hers, his heart pounding a frantic rhythm against his ribs. Ishita met his eyes, her expression thoughtful.

"Anesh," she began, her voice soft yet firm, "yes. I think I do too. You've always treated me with respect, even when I rejected you before. You never pressured me, and that means a lot."

A warm smile bloomed on Anesh's face. "I wouldn't dream of it," he said, his voice thick with relief. "Honestly, Ishita, I can't imagine spending my life with anyone else."

Their conversation flowed late into the night, filled with laughter and whispered secrets. As the first rays of dawn painted the sky, Anesh reluctantly walked Ishita home, their fingers brushing as they said their goodbyes. A spark had ignited that night, a flicker of hope amidst the darkness they'd both been navigating.

The following days unfolded like a dream. Late-night conversations became a cherished ritual, their voices filling the phone lines with a newfound intimacy. Daily visits turned into a delightful routine, filled with stolen glances, shared laughter, and a growing sense of belonging. Spending time together became the cornerstone of their lives. They explored hidden corners of the city, their conversations flowing effortlessly as they discovered new things about each other.

Anesh, ever the charmer, surprised Ishita with small tokens of affection – a single perfect rose, a handwritten note tucked into her bag, a book he knew she'd been wanting to read. Ishita, in turn, reciprocated with thoughtful gestures of her own – a scarf she'd knitted for him, tickets to a concert they'd both spoken of attending, a framed photo capturing a particularly joyous moment during one of their outings.

Their bond deepened with each passing day. They confided in each other, sharing their vulnerabilities and dreams, their fears and aspirations. Anesh learned about Ishita's passion for photography, her secret desire to travel the world. Ishita discovered Anesh's love for writing, his hidden talent for playing the guitar. They reveled in these discoveries, their connection strengthening with each shared secret.

Through it all, their love blossomed, a testament to the power of second chances and the healing touch of time. Theirs wasn't a fairy-tale romance, but a real, relatable journey – a messy, beautiful tapestry woven with threads of joy, sorrow, forgiveness, and acceptance. As they walked together towards their future, a future they were now painting together, they knew their love story was just beginning.

Anesh had built his happiness on a foundation of sand. His carefully constructed facade, the image of the caring friend, the devoted boyfriend, was about to crumble. Karma, it seemed, had a wicked sense of timing.

Psychowrath

One day, the unexpected phone call shattered the illusion of peace Anesh had so desperately craved. It was Ruhi, the ghost from his past, the one who had vanished after Sandy's death. A knot of dread tightened in his stomach. What did she want now?

He picked up the call, his voice strained. "Ruhi?"

Her voice, laced with a dangerous edge, crackled through the receiver. "Enjoying your newfound bliss, Anesh? Living happily ever after you stole from my family?"

Anesh's carefully constructed smile faltered. "Ruhi, what are you talking about?"

"Don't play dumb, Anesh," she spat. "I know everything. You, the perfect boyfriend, the grieving friend – a master of disguise. But your mask is slipping, Anesh. You're a killer."

The blood drained from Anesh's face. The carefully buried secrets, the truth he'd locked away, threatened to erupt. "Killer? What are you...?"

"You murdered Sandeep bhaiya," Ruhi cut him off, her voice thick with accusation. "You thought you could get away with it, hide behind your innocent facade. But I saw you, Anesh. The morning after bhaiya died, at that cafe. I knew then there was more to the story."

The world seemed to tilt on its axis. Ruhi had seen him? Had she pieced together the truth all along? Panic clawed at his throat.

"I've been collecting proof, Anesh," Ruhi continued, her voice colder than winter. "Month after month, building a case against you. And now, you're cornered. Meet me near the abandoned building by the highway."

Ruhi, consumed by grief and rage, didn't understand the depths of Anesh's darkness. But Anesh knew. He knew the monster he was, the cunning predator lurking beneath the surface. And for the first time, he truly feared the consequences of his actions. Trapped between denial and dread, Anesh agreed to meet Ruhi, a knot of foreboding twisting in his gut. He knew this wasn't just a meeting; it was a reckoning.

The late afternoon sun beat down on Anesh's car as he cruised towards the abandoned building. The highway stretched out before him, a deserted ribbon of asphalt leading to his destination. In the distance, the building jutted up like a jagged tooth against the clear blue sky. It wasn't exactly a luxury resort, but it would have to do.

As Anesh turned off the highway and onto the dirt road, the silence became almost too quiet. Just the crunch of tires on gravel, a sound that echoed in the stillness. The air hung heavy, thick with the smell of something past its prime and a faint metallic tang that tickled his nose. Nothing out of the ordinary for an abandoned building.

This wasn't Anesh's first time playing this kind of game. Sure, the building looked creepy — all rusted metal and crumbling concrete, like a forgotten toy left to rot in the sandbox. Cobwebs, thick and dusty, clung to the skeletal remains of vines that made a half-hearted attempt to reclaim the place for nature. But hey, a little rust never hurts anyone.

The closer he got, the building seemed to shrink a bit, like a giant taking a deep breath before a fight. Cracks snaked across the walls, more like decoration than anything dangerous. Chunks of paint peeled away, revealing the boring concrete underneath. A few loose sheets of metal clattered in the wind; a rusty song Anesh barely registered.

The entrance was a gaping hole, like a giant's missing tooth. Weeds choked the threshold, but that was just nature reclaiming its space. Inside, shadows played hide-and-seek in the fading light, nothing a good phone flashlight couldn't handle.

This wasn't a haunted house or a spooky movie set. This was just a place to get down to business. A place where the shadows held secrets.

Suddenly, a sharp crack echoed as something slammed into the back of his head. The world tilted, and Anesh hit the floor with a surprised yelp. He groaned, vision swimming as he rolled onto his back. Through the blur, a figure emerged from the shadows. It was Ruhi, her face twisted with rage. Her eyes, usually warm, now burned with a cold fire.

Anesh gasped for breath, the metallic tang of blood filling his mouth. "Ruhi," he rasped, his voice choked with fear. "Ruhi, listen to me!"

But Ruhi's eyes blazed with a fury that eclipsed all reason. "Don't you dare speak my name!" she screamed. "You took my brother away, and now you'll pay." She raised the object in her hand – a rusted pipe, glinting menacingly in the dim light – and lunged at him again.

Anesh threw his arm up in a futile attempt to shield himself, but the blow landed with a sickening thud. Blood streamed down his face, blurring his vision. He coughed, a strangled sound that echoed in the vast emptiness of the building.

"There's no truth left for you to tell, Anesh," Ruhi snarled, her voice laced with ice. "You murdered my brother, and now you'll face the consequences."

Desperation clawed at Anesh. He knew he had to make her listen, somehow. "Wait, Ruhi!" he wheezed. "It was an accident, I swear! I never meant to hurt him. I just..." He trailed off, searching for the right words that might pierce through her rage.

"You just what?" Ruhi challenged, her voice trembling with barely contained emotion. "You just decided to take his life on a whim?"

Shame burned in Anesh's gut, a searing counterpoint to the physical pain throbbing in his head. "No," he forced out, his voice barely a whisper. "I came to see Sandy that night… to tell him about us. About how I felt for you, Ruhi. I knew you cared for me, but I was scared. I thought maybe, if I talked to him, everything would be okay."

Ruhi scoffed, a harsh, disbelieving sound. "Don't try to play me, Anesh. You think a pretty lie will erase what you've done?"

Ruhi's rage hung heavy in the air, a thick fog threatening to drown Anesh. He knew there was no escape, no smooth-talking his way out of this. With a heavy sigh, he spoke, his voice hoarse.

"Ruhi, listen to me," he pleaded. "I know you want me dead. Maybe you're right. Maybe I deserve it after taking your brother away from you."

A flicker of pain crossed Ruhi's face, a brief crack in her armor. Anesh pressed on; his voice laced with a desperation that bordered on believability.

"When I told him about us, he wasn't Sandy" he said. "He was furious, Ruhi. He threatened me, said he'd kill me. I tried to calm him down, but he wouldn't listen. He shoved me, and I fell hard on the ground. He grabbed a gardening tool, a spade I think, and swung it at my head. It missed, thank God, but it got my hand. Those bandages that you saw, that's where the blood came from."

He paused, his eyes searching hers for a flicker of doubt, anything to suggest she might be listening. "I was scared, Ruhi. Terrified. All I could think about was you, your beautiful face. But I didn't hurt him. I fought back, but I just wanted to get away."

Anesh's voice grew lower, a tremor of fear creeping in. "Your dog, Tyson, he chased me. Cornered me. Sandy came after me too, but then…" his voice trailed off, a calculated hesitation. "There was a fire, out in the field. Somehow, Sandy was on his motorbike, and it caught fire, the flames spreading fast. Tyson… he got caught too in saving Sandy."

He looked at Ruhi, his face etched with fabricated remorse. "I was hurt, lying on the ground. I couldn't do anything. All I could see was them burning."

Anesh's words were carefully chosen, a web of truth and lies designed to shift the blame, to paint himself as the victim caught in a tragic accident.

Ruhi's voice crackled with barely contained fury. "Don't play dumb, Anesh. If you truly cared about any of this, why didn't you come forward? Why not confess to the police? Explain yourself!"

Anesh stammered, the bravado he'd arrived with evaporating under Ruhi's fierce gaze. "I... I was scared," he mumbled, his voice barely a whisper. "I thought they wouldn't believe me. You were the only one who could understand, but you were so devastated by Sandy's death... I thought you wouldn't listen. So, I stayed quiet."

Ruhi's eyes narrowed. "And what about this little charade with Ishita? Was that an accident too?"

Anesh flinched. "No, not exactly. Things got complicated. Ishita kind of forced me into this relationship. After Samaira died, she threatened to tell the police that Samaira took her own life because I rejected her. And after Sandy… well, I feared the police. I just went along with it."

Ruhi stared at him, a mix of disbelief and dawning realization flickering in her eyes. "But..." her voice trailed off, the accusation in her eyes wavering.

Anesh seized the opportunity. "Ruhi, listen to me," he said, his voice filled with forced sincerity. "I've told you everything, the whole truth. I feel awful about what happened, and I wouldn't blame you for hating me. But it was an accident, a terrible accident. Sandy's death weighs heavy on my heart too."

Ruhi's gaze held him for a long moment, searching for any flicker of deceit. Slowly, a hint of belief softened her features. "Anesh," she whispered, her voice thick with emotion, "I… I think I believe you. I'm so sorry I ever suspected you of hurting him deliberately."

An imperceptible smile played on Anesh's lips. His carefully constructed web of lies seemed to be holding. Relief washed over him, a cold, calculating satisfaction. He had manipulated Ruhi's grief, turning her anger into a shield for his own crimes.

"Thank you, Ruhi," he said, his voice dripping with false remorse. "That means a lot to me."

Ruhi, consumed by regret, didn't notice the emptiness in his eyes. "Here, let me get you some water," she offered, hurrying towards a shadowy corner of the building.

As she moved away, Anesh took a moment to compose himself. The encounter had been a tightrope walk, but he had emerged unscathed. Ruhi, blinded by her grief and his carefully crafted performance, was putty in his hands. A dangerous glint flickered in his eyes. This wasn't over. He still had loose ends to tie up, and Ruhi, unknowingly, had just become part of his twisted game.

In that split second, Anesh saw his opportunity. With a surge of adrenaline, he lunged. Ruhi cried out in surprise as he slammed into her, sending them both crashing to the floor. He wasted no time, raining down blows with a chilling ferocity.

Ruhi, caught off guard and overwhelmed by the sudden attack, crumpled beneath him. Pain lanced through her body, tears stinging her eyes. "You... you lied to me," she gasped, her voice hoarse with betrayal. "You're a monster! I should never have trusted you."

Anesh, his face contorted in a grotesque parody of a smile, leaned close. "See, Ruhi," he purred, his voice dripping with malice. "I always say girls are too easily swayed by emotions. And here you are, proving me right."

Her pleas for help fell on deaf ears. He secured her to a thick metal pole with practiced efficiency, a horrifying calmness replacing his earlier bravado. Then, with a cold, calculating glint in his eyes, he retrieved a container from his car – kerosene. With practiced ease, he began dousing the building in the flammable liquid, a cruel smile twisting his lips.

Ruhi watched in horror, a primal scream clawing its way up her throat. Trapped and helpless, the acrid scent of kerosene filling her nostrils, she knew this was the end. Tears streamed down her face as the flames, ignited by a flick of his lighter, began to lick hungrily at the walls. The building, once a silent giant, roared to life with a wall of fire.

Anesh cast one final, emotionless glance at Ruhi. A cold, cruel laugh escaped his lips, echoing eerily in the inferno that was now the abandoned building. With a final flourish, he turned and disappeared into the night, leaving Ruhi to her fate. Smoke choked the air, stinging her eyes and filling her lungs with a burning despair. Tears blurred her vision, her screams swallowed by the hungry roar of the flames. Trapped and helpless, she knew this was the end.

But then, through the haze of smoke and despair, a flicker of movement caught Ruhi's fading eyesight. She blinked, forcing her heavy eyelids to open a sliver. Was it just a trick of the dying light? A figment of her overheating mind? She squinted, focusing on the shadowy figure near the entrance of the building. It seemed to be moving closer, its form solidifying through the smoke.

Hope, a fragile ember, flickered to life within Ruhi. Could it be? Could someone has seen the flames, heard her screams? But the world was a blur, and her thoughts were muddled. Was this just another cruel illusion conjured by the fire?

The figure continued to approach, its form taking shape. It was a man, tall and broad-shouldered, silhouetted against the flickering inferno. Ruhi didn't recognize him, his features hidden in the smoke and the encroaching darkness. Yet, a sliver of hope, fragile as a spider's thread, stretched within her.

"Hello?" she croaked, her voice a hoarse whisper. The man stopped, his head snapping towards her. A tense silence hung heavy in the air, broken only by the crackling flames. Ruhi strained to see his face, her heart hammering a frantic tattoo against her ribs.

"Ruhi?" the man knew her name, his voice deep and urgent. It cut through the haze; a lifeline thrown towards her. This was real. Help had arrived. She was amazed, who could it be?

With a surge of adrenaline, Ruhi tried to scream, to call out for help. But her throat was raw, her voice a pathetic rasp that died in the swirling smoke. Tears streamed down her face, a mixture of relief and despair. She was trapped, her body weak and burning.

The man, his face now etched with concern, moved closer. He took in the scene – the raging fire, the bound figure struggling against the metal pole. Understanding dawned on his features, a grim determination replacing the initial surprise.

"Don't worry," he called out, his voice barely audible over the roar of the fire. "I'm going to get you out of there!"

Ruhi watched with desperate hope as the man, with surprising agility, began navigating the burning building. He dodged fallen debris and flaming timbers, his movements sure and purposeful. Each step he took closer to her seemed like an eternity.

He reached the metal pole, his form momentarily obscured by a thick plume of smoke. Ruhi held her breath, fear and anticipation warring within her. Then, he emerged, a fire extinguisher clutched in his hand. With practiced efficiency, he doused the flames that danced around her, creating a small pocket of breathable air.

"I need you to hold on tight," he shouted, his voice muffled by the mask covering his face. Ruhi, fueled by a sudden surge of strength, nodded frantically. He knelt beside her, his movements swift and precise as he began to cut through the metal bindings with a tool he seemed to materialize out of thin air.

Every second felt like an hour, the heat licking at their exposed skin. The fire, momentarily subdued, seemed to gather its strength, the flames reaching hungrily towards them. Ruhi could hear the crackle and hiss as the inferno devoured the building around them.

Finally, with a satisfying snap, the metal bindings gave way. The man, wasting no time, scooped Ruhi up in his arms. She clung to him desperately, her body weak and trembling. He turned, his eyes scanning the room for an escape route.

"There!" he yelled, pointing towards a hidden door partially obscured by debris. It was a gamble, a chance they had to take. With Ruhi held tight against him, he sprinted towards the door, pushing through the burning debris that blocked their path.

They burst through the doorway, collapsing onto the cool grass outside just as the roof of the building caved in with a deafening roar. The night sky, now ablaze with the reflection of the inferno, seemed to hold its breath for a moment, before a fierce wind whipped past them, carrying the stench of burning wood and despair.

Ruhi lay there, gasping for air, her body a symphony of aches and tremors. Every breath felt like a victory, every beat of her heart a testament to her sheer will to survive. Though pain pulsed through her like a relentless drumbeat, a sliver of gratitude sliced through the fog of exhaustion. She was alive. She had somehow escaped the fiery maw of the collapsing building, snatched from the clutches of death at the very last moment.

Tears, a mixture of relief and something deeper, streamed down her smoke-stained face. Through eyes blurred by pain and caked with soot, she looked up at the man who had become her unlikely savior. He knelt beside her, his presence a stark contrast to the devastation that surrounded them.

Unlike the wiry frame she'd expected of a local villager who might have stumbled upon the inferno, this man was built like a seasoned warrior. Broad shoulders strained beneath a fire-resistant jacket, hinting at a powerful physique. But it wasn't just his physical strength that captivated her attention. There was an air of quiet competence about him, an effortless grace in the way he moved despite the chaos that had just unfolded.

His face, partially obscured by the mask that had filtered the smoke during their escape, was young, no older than twenty-one at most. A mop of dark hair, tousled by the wind, framed features that were both rugged and captivating. Strong brows were furrowed in concern, and beneath them, a pair of eyes, the color of a stormy sea, held a depth that sent shivers down her spine.

But it was the way he looked at her, not with pity or surprise, but with a startling intensity that truly unsettled her. It was an intensity that spoke of something more – a hint of recognition, a flicker of something she couldn't quite decipher.

"You're safe now," he said, his voice a low rumble that vibrated through her. It wasn't the voice of a local villager, but one seasoned by experience, laced with an accent, she couldn't quite place. Who was he? Where did he come from? And how, in this remote part of the world, did he know her name? The questions swirled in her mind, a tangled web that threatened to unravel the fragile thread of her newfound safety.

Chapter Five: A Known Stranger

God always offers us a second chance in life.

~Paulo Coelho

Ruhi blinked, her vision blurry as she struggled to focus. The world tilted with each shallow breath, the aftermath of her ordeal a dull ache throbbing through her limbs. A low, reassuring rumble cut through the haze clouding her mind.

She tried to lift her head, wincing as a spike of agony shot through her skull. A hand, strong and calloused, gently nudged her back down.

"Easy," he murmured, his voice close to her ear. "Take it slow."

With a supreme effort, Ruhi managed to pry open her eyelids. Light, dappled and filtered through leaves, streamed down on her. They were nestled beneath a large oak tree, its gnarled branches forming a protective canopy overhead. Her savior knelt beside her, his presence a silent reassurance. Curiosity gnawed at the edges of her fear. She stole a glance at him, surprised by what she saw.

Dark hair, windswept from their recent escape, framed a face that defied easy definition. High cheekbones accentuated a lean jawline, the strong features softened by a pair of mesmerizing eyes. Their color, a stormy grey flecked with green, mirrored the roiling emotions swirling within him. Concern etched lines around their edges, a stark contrast to the harsh lines etched permanently onto his skin.

A jagged scar, a pale lightning bolt that started at his temple and zig-zagged down to his jawline, marred the smooth perfection of his face. It was an old scar, the raised edges softened by time, but the story it held remained untold. Another, newer scar, a deep red gash across the back of his hand, spoke of a recent struggle, a battle won but not unscathed.

He wore a simple black t-shirt stretched taut across broad shoulders; the fabric torn at the sleeve revealing a glimpse of toned muscle beneath. Dark cargo pants, stained with mud and grime, hung low on his hips.

But beneath the rough exterior, Ruhi sensed a hidden strength, a quiet resilience that had seen him through countless battles. His eyes, though guarded, held a spark of kindness that ignited a flicker of trust within her.

"Who are you?" she rasped, her voice a mere croak.

He didn't answer immediately, his gaze fixed on a point beyond the trees. A muscle flexed involuntarily in his jaw, betraying the turmoil churning beneath the surface. Finally, he met her eyes, his gaze steady and unwavering.

"My name is Ishank," he said, his voice a low monotone, a stark contrast to the chaos that had just unfolded.

The name hit Ruhi like a bolt of lightning. "Ishank?" she croaked, her voice a rasp. Disbelief battled with a flicker of hope in her eyes. "But you're... you're dead. Anesh told me..."

A flicker of something unreadable crossed Ishank's face, a storm brewing beneath the surface of his calm exterior. "It was all a lie," he said, his voice hardening. "Anesh tried to kill me that night."

Ruhi's breath hitched. The pieces of the puzzle began to fall into place. The sudden accident of his brother, the grief that had choked her, the anger simmering just beneath the surface — it all made a horrifying sense.

"He pushed me off a cliff," Ishank continued, his voice laced with a barely controlled rage. "But somehow, I ended up by the river. Some villagers found me... unconscious." He hesitated, a shadow flickering across his eyes. "I was in a coma for two years."

"I woke up a few weeks ago," Ishank went on, his gaze fixed on the smoldering ruins of the building. "In a stranger's room. They told me about the coma, the lost years."

He turned to face her, his eyes burning with a fierce intensity. "I had to get back home, to see my family. But I knew I couldn't let Anesh know I was alive. He'd be... cautious. He'd try to finish what he started."

Ruhi understood. Anesh, the charming friend, the pillar of support – a monster in disguise. The weight of his betrayal pressed down on her, choking her with a fresh wave of anger.

"I told my parents not to tell anyone," Ishank said, his voice a low growl.

Ruhi, her voice barely a whisper, asked, "How did you find out about me? How did you know that I am here in this desolate place, suffering, crying out for help?"

Ishank, his voice steady, answered, "I've been tracking Anesh for several weeks now. I discovered the shocking truth about Sandy's murder and subsequently, Samaira's. Both were victims of Anesh's ruthless machinations."

Ruhi, interrupting Ishank, stammered, "Samaira's murder?" The words felt strange on her tongue - an unthinkable reality.

Ishank nodded gravely. "Yes, Ruhi. Samaira's death wasn't a suicide as everyone believed. She was yet another pawn in Anesh's deadly game. He murdered her because she dared to come between him and Ishita. The same fate befell Sandy."

At the mention of her brother's name, Ruhi's heart ached. Her eyes, glistening with unshed tears, blazed with an anger so fierce it was palpable. "We cannot let this monster claim another life. It ends here," she declared, her voice trembling with resolve.

Ishank agreed fervently. "I've been strategizing against him, Ruhi. I've been watching his every move, biding my time. I'm hell-bent on making sure he pays for his heinous crimes. He won't slip through the cracks, not under my watch. But I need you by my side for this, Ruhi. Anesh is cunning; defeating him won't be a walk in the park."

"We need to get back," Ishank said, his voice hardening with resolve. "I need to see Ishita, and we need to warn her about Anesh." He held out a hand to help her up, his touch surprisingly gentle despite the callouses that marred his skin.

The tension between them was electric. The stakes were high, and the task daunting. But both knew that they had to stop Anesh, no matter the cost. The path ahead was fraught with danger and uncertainty, but they were ready to face it, united in their mission to bring justice for Samaira and Sandy. The story of their fight against Anesh was just beginning, and it promised to be one marked by courage, determination, and an unyielding pursuit of justice.

Psychowrath

College vacations had begun, and Anesh had a plan up his sleeve. He decided to whisk Ishita away to his hometown, a decision he kept under wraps, not even confiding in their parents. He arranged for their stay, and Ishita, smitten by Anesh's charm, agreed without a second thought.

In stark contrast, Ishank was aware of Anesh's intentions of taking Ishita with him, but the specific location eluded him. He shared his past with Ishita with Ruhi, expressing his concerns about her future being tainted by Anesh's sinister plans.

Undeterred by the lack of approval or awareness of their parents, Anesh and Ishita embarked on their vacation, heading to the place of Anesh's choosing.

Simultaneously, Ishank and Ruhi embarked on their investigation, and their combined efforts bore fruit, revealing the hidden location of Anesh and Ishita.

Ishank turned to Ruhi, gratitude etched on his face, "Ruhi, I can't thank you enough for your help. I promise to avenge your brother's death and save Ishita from that lunatic, Anesh."

"But I'm coming with you," Ruhi interjected swiftly. "This isn't your battle alone."

Ishank's face reflected concern, "There's a lot of risk involved, Ruhi. It would be safer for you to stay here.

Also, what would you tell your parents? Would they agree?"

"I'll tell them it's for a college project," Ruhi replied, determination gleaming in her eyes.

Ishank conceded, "Okay, as you wish."

Together, they embarked on their journey, reaching the quaint town of Kasauli, the place where everything began. Two years had passed but Kasauli remained largely unchanged. The air still held the crisp mountain chill, and the iconic Christ Church perched proudly on the hilltop, a silent sentinel against the changing tides of time. The winding lanes, lined with shops selling local handicrafts and cafes offering steaming cups of chai, seemed frozen in a familiar embrace. Yet, a subtle shift hung in the atmosphere, a weight of worry replacing the carefree joy that once permeated their memories.

Ishank and Ruhi found themselves embroiled in an intricate game of cat and mouse, keeping a vigilant eye on Anesh. They keenly observed his daily activities, scrutinizing his every move. A meticulous plan was being woven against him and they patiently bid their time, waiting for the opportune moment to serve him his just desserts.

One day, Anesh, oblivious to their scrutiny, left his abode to run some errands. Seizing this golden opportunity, Ishank and Ruhi made their way to the residence where Anesh and Ishita were staying.

Ishank, his heart pounding in anticipation, rang the doorbell. Inside, Ishita was startled by the unexpected sound. She wondered, 'Who could it be at this hour?'

As she opened the door, she found herself staring at a familiar face, a face that belonged to her past. There, standing in front of her was Ishank, a known stranger. The sight turned her world on its head. Memories, long suppressed, came rushing back, a torrent of emotions that left her reeling. She could hardly believe her eyes; it was nothing short of a miracle. Ishank, her first love, was back. It was a moment of pure joy and profound confusion.

Amid her emotional turmoil, a harsh reality dawned on her - her relationship with Anesh. The joy of reuniting with Ishank was overshadowed by the grim reality of her present relationship. Her heart ached, torn between her past love and her current commitment. On one hand, there was Ishank, her long-lost love, who had resurfaced from the depths of her memories, and on the other, there was Anesh, who had filled her life with promises of happiness and joy. She found herself at a crossroad, a situation she had never envisioned.

Ishita, taken aback by the sudden appearance of Ishank and Ruhi, managed to extend a shaky welcome. She wasn't particularly close to Ruhi; however, she recognized her from their shared time in college. She ushered them in, offering them a seat.

"Ishita," Ishank began, his voice steady despite the urgency of the situation, "I know your mind must be a whirlwind of confusion and questions right now, but time is of the essence. We need to leave before Anesh returns."

Ruhi chimed in, "Yes, Ishita. We're here to warn you about Anesh. There's more to the story, but this place isn't safe for such revelations. Find a way to meet us tomorrow at the local chai shop down the lane, around 4 pm."

"But...what's happened?" Ishita's voice wavered, "Why are you warning me against Anesh? What has he done?"

"For now," Ishank said, his gaze intense, "all I can tell you is that Anesh poses a grave danger to all of us. We must take our leave now. Please meet us as planned tomorrow. And remember, Anesh mustn't know we were here."

Suddenly Anesh came and as he opened the door, he immediately sensed something was amiss. There was a lingering unfamiliar scent in the air and a barely perceptible tension that hung heavy in the room. His eyes narrowed in suspicion as he questioned Ishita about any visitors.

Meanwhile, Ishank and Ruhi, who had been hiding in the adjacent room, heard Anesh's voice. Their hearts pounded in their chests as they realized they needed to leave immediately without alerting Anesh.

Ishita, managing to keep her voice steady, denied any visitors. Anesh's suspicious gaze did not escape her notice, causing her heart to pound louder in her chest.

Seeing Anesh's suspicion, Ishank and Ruhi knew they had to act swiftly. They waited for a moment when Anesh was occupied, and then, with soft, measured steps, they made their way to the back door. Their exit was as silent as their entry, leaving no trace of their visit.

Anesh, still doubtful, decided to brush his suspicions aside. He smiled at Ishita, dismissing his earlier question as a joke. Ishita breathed a sigh of relief as the tension eased, her heart rate gradually returning to normal, and the day continued as if nothing unusual had happened.

However, the meeting with Ishank and Ruhi had planted seeds of doubt and fear in Ishita's mind about Anesh. Their sudden arrival left her in a state of bewilderment. She was left with a myriad of unanswered questions and a sense of dread about Anesh. This feeling was amplified when Anesh returned home earlier than expected. The suspense and anticipation of the upcoming meeting at the chai shop left her with a restlessness that was impossible to ignore.

As the day broke, events began to unfold exactly as planned. Ishita found herself meeting with Ishank and Ruhi, who both donned eccentric outfits, complete with a cap and hat respectively. Their peculiar attire was a deliberate attempt to evade Anesh's attention. Ishita joined them at their table, her heart pounding with anticipation.

"Ishita," Ishank started, his voice serious and low, "What we're about to reveal is grave, so I need your undivided attention. Anesh isn't the man you perceive him to be. His affections for you have been built atop a mountain of horrific deeds."

He paused, letting the weight of his words sink in before continuing, "He attacked me first. I was fortunate enough to survive. The night of my accident wasn't an accident at all. Anesh orchestrated it, pushing me from a cliff to eliminate me from your life."

Ruhi took over, her eyes brimming with a mix of fear and anger, "That wasn't all. He murdered my brother when he grew suspicious of your friendship with Sandeep. He set my brother ablaze, simply because he was close to you, Ishita."

A heavy silence followed before Ishank spoke again, "Your best friend Samaira didn't commit suicide. Anesh was aware that you'd never accept his proposal if you knew Samaira was in love with him. So, he murdered her. And when Ruhi attempted to avenge her brother, he tried to kill her too. I managed to intervene just in time."

Ishita's face was a mask of disbelief, "I can't believe you two. How could Anesh, such a gentle soul, be capable of such atrocities? It seems to me, Ishank, that you're just envious of our bond and can't bear to see it thrive."

Ruhi interjected, her tone steady, "We knew it wouldn't be easy to convince you. That's why I've gathered substantial evidence against him."

Ruhi's collection of proofs was damning, convincing enough to shatter Ishita's illusions. Overwhelmed, she cursed her fate, tears welling up in her eyes as the harsh reality of Anesh's monstrous deeds came crashing down on her.

Tears streamed down Ishita's face, blurring the world around her. "What do we do now?" she choked out, her voice thick with grief and burgeoning fear.

Ishank, his eyes glittering with a dangerous intensity, knelt beside her. "The police won't help us here, Ishita," he said, his voice low and cold. "This is about more than just a fight. This is about you, my love, the love Anesh stole from me. And this is about justice for Samaira."

Ruhi, her own face etched with a chilling resolve, placed a comforting hand on Ishita's shoulder. "He'll pay, Ishita," she said fiercely. "I watched my family crumble after my brother died. Anesh won't just go to jail. He deserves worse."

Ishita recoiled slightly, a tremor of unease running through her. The raw pain of their loss, the betrayal they felt, twisted their grief into something dark and ominous.

"We'll go back tomorrow, to your place," Ishank continued, his voice a steely whisper. "And this time, Ishita, it ends." The weight of his words hung heavy in the air. Ishita, numb with shock and a growing sense of dread, simply nodded.

The following day unfolded exactly as planned. Ishank and Ruhi, their faces etched with nervous anticipation, arrived at the secluded cabin where Anesh was staying. Ishita welcomed them and Anesh was nowhere to be seen.

In the corner of the cabin, shrouded by a dim light, they joined each other, their faces masked by shadows.

Ishank's dark eyes were intense, and his voice was low when he started speaking, "The plan is simple. We need to be calm and careful. He cannot suspect anything."

Ishita, her hands trembling slightly, nodded. "We need to make it look like an accident," she said, her voice barely audible.

Ruhi, the youngest amongst them, clenched her fists, her eyes gleaming with a strange determination. "We can tamper with his car... loosen some bolts or something," she suggested, the cruel reality of their plan making her voice quiver.

Ishank considered this, his gaze far off. "Yes, but we need to make sure it's untraceable," he added, the gravity of their situation sinking in.

In hushed tones, they huddled near the back door, finalizing their desperate plan - to stop Anesh before he went any further. Each of them carried the weight of their decision, a grim acceptance of the path they had chosen.

Suddenly, the front door creaked open. Anesh's voice, laced with a chilling calmness, rang out. "Ishita?"

He came earlier than expected. Ishita's heart lurched. Fear, cold and sharp, clawed at her throat. She forced a smile, her voice barely a whisper when she replied, "Anesh, it's me." She went close to the door, the echo of their plan still ringing in her ears.

He didn't enter. Instead, he reached through the doorway, his grip like a vice on her hand. With a swift jerk, he pulled her outside, slamming the door shut behind them with a sickening thud.

Panic flared in Ishita's eyes. "Anesh, what are you doing?" she stammered, her voice trembling.

A cruel smile played on his lips. He held up a small, black object – a remote control. "Playing a little game, Ishita," he said, his voice devoid of warmth. "Seems you and your little team underestimated me."

"What team?" Ishita's voice cracked. Her mind raced, desperately trying to piece together his words.

Anesh's gaze hardened. "Don't play dumb, Ishita. I saw you yesterday, whispering with Ishank and Ruhi down the lane. Plotting your little revenge, were you?"

A wave of nausea washed over Ishita. So, he knew. It was all out in the open now. "Anesh, please," she pleaded, tears welling up in her eyes. "There's been a misunderstanding. We just… we wanted to talk to you."

He scoffed. "Talk? Or stop me? You think I don't know what you've been planning? Last time, maybe your friends got lucky. But this time, there'll be no saving them."

His words echoed in the stillness of the night; each syllable heavy with menace. Ishank and Ruhi, hidden around the corner, exchanged a horrified glance. Their carefully laid plan was falling apart, their worst fears confirmed.

"What are you talking about?" Ishita whispered, her voice thick with dread.

Anesh's smile stretched wider, sending shivers down her spine. "See this?" He brandished the remote in front of her face. "It controls a little device I rigged up inside the cabin. A silent killer, you might say."

Ishita's breath hitched. "Carbon monoxide?" she whispered, the words tasting like ash in her mouth.

Anesh chuckled, a humorless sound devoid of warmth. "Bingo. In about an hour, that cabin will be filled with it. And your precious Ishank and Ruhi… well, let's just say their time will be up."

A strangled sob escaped Ishita's lips. This wasn't the Anesh she knew, the quiet boy who sat beside her in class, the friend who helped her catch up on missed work. This was a stranger, his eyes filled with a chilling darkness.

"Anesh, please," she begged, desperation lacing her voice. "They're your friends too. Don't do this. There has to be another way."

Anesh's face contorted in a sneer. "Friends? They are planning to kill me."

Anesh yanked Ishita towards the car, shoving her roughly into the passenger seat. Panic clawed at her throat as the car lurched forward, tires spitting gravel as they sped away from that place.

Anesh gripped the steering wheel, knuckles white, as he sped towards Ishank's house, he knew that Ishank must have told everything about him to his parents and they could be a threat to his life.

He slammed on the brakes, the car screeching to a halt in the middle of the deserted road. A police car, its blue lights flashing like malevolent eyes, had appeared in the distance. Panic clawed at his throat. He couldn't be caught. Not now. With a desperate jerk, he threw the car into a U-turn, tires squealing in protest.

Then he saw him. Mr. Kapoor, the very same detective who had interrogated him after Samaira's death, sat behind the wheel of the approaching car. Anesh's stomach lurched. This was bad. This was very bad.

Mr. Kapoor spotted him too, his face set in a grim determination. He slammed his foot on the accelerator, his car a relentless predator in hot pursuit. Adrenaline surged through Anesh's veins. He knew these mountain roads like the back of his hand, every turn, every hidden dip. He pushed the car to its limits, weaving through narrow passes, his tires flirting with the edge of sheer drops.

The chase went on for what felt like hours, the sun sinking lower in the sky, painting the mountains in hues of orange and red. But Mr. Kapoor was relentless, his car doggedly pursuing him. Anesh's heart hammered against his ribs, a frantic drumbeat against the roar of the engine.

Finally, exhaustion began to set in. His arms ached, his vision blurred at the edges. He needed an escape, a way to break free. He spotted a sharp turn ahead, a narrow switchback that led to a secluded clearing at the mountain's peak. It was a risky maneuver, but his only option.

With a deep breath, Anesh slammed on the brakes and yanked the steering wheel, his tires screeching in protest. The car lurched and skidded, threatening to topple over the edge. He fought for control, his heart pounding a frantic tattoo against his ribs. He managed to straighten the car, but just barely.

He pulled into the clearing, his chest heaving with exertion. But the triumph was short-lived. Mr. Kapoor's car appeared moments later, blocking his escape. Anesh was trapped, cornered like a frightened animal.

He shut off the engine, the sudden silence oppressive. A tense stillness hung in the air, broken only by the rasping of his own breath. He climbed out of the car, his legs shaky, his hands raised in a desperate plea.

"Mr. Kapoor," he croaked, his voice dry with fear. "Look, we can talk about this. It's a misunderstanding."

Mr. Kapoor emerged from his car, his face grim. Months seemed to have etched themselves onto his features, the lines deeper, the eyes a steely gray. But a flicker of recognition burned within them.

"Anesh," he said, his voice low and steady. "So, my hunch was right. You do have a lot to answer for."

Anesh's mind raced. He had to get out of this. He had to manipulate his way out, just like always. "Mr. Kapoor," he pleaded, desperation creeping into his voice. "There's an explanation. You just need to hear me out."

Mr. Kapoor studied him for a long moment, his gaze unwavering. "I don't think so, Anesh," he finally said. "The game is up. You're coming with me."

He reached into his pocket, his hand emerging with a pair of handcuffs. Fear, primal and raw, flooded Anesh. He couldn't go to jail. He couldn't face the consequences of his actions.

Psychowrath

In a desperate lunge, he lunged for Mr. Kapoor, a primal scream ripping from his throat. He caught the detective off guard, knocking him backward. With a sickening thud, Mr. Kapoor landed on the rocky ground, his gun flying from his holster.

Anesh scrambled for the weapon, his mind a whirlwind of panic. He couldn't let Mr. Kapoor get to it first. Before he could think twice, he had the gun in his hand, the cold metal a foreign sensation against his skin.

He pointed the weapon at Mr. Kapoor, who lay there stunned, his eyes wide with disbelief. For a moment, a flicker of something akin to humanity flickered in Anesh's eyes. Shame? Regret? It was impossible to tell. But the moment was fleeting, extinguished by the cold, calculating glint that returned.

"Don't move," he rasped, his voice barely a whisper. The gun felt heavy in his hand, a symbol of the power he craved, the power he'd stop at nothing to retain.

Mr. Kapoor, ever the detective, remained calm. "Anesh," he said, his voice steady despite the tremor in his hands. "This doesn't have to be like this. You can still walk away from this."

Anesh scoffed. "Walk away? After everything I've done? Don't be ridiculous." His finger tightened on the trigger, a morbid fascination playing out in his eyes. "You see, Mr. Kapoor, some games can only end one way."

A single, deafening shot shattered the mountain silence. Mr. Kapoor's body crumpled to the ground, a crimson stain blooming on his chest. Anesh stared at the gun in his hand, a cold emptiness washing over him. He had crossed a line, killed an on-duty officer.

Frustration gnawed at Anesh as he reached Ishank's home. Ishank's house stood empty; a hollow shell devoid of life. The windows were dark, no sign of movement within. An unsettling premonition coiled in his gut.

Had Ishank anticipated this? Had he moved them, his family, to safety, sensing the danger that lurked in the shadows?

Chapter Six: The Last Laugh

What goes around comes around.

~Anonymous

While Anesh was busy in his encounter with Mr. Kapoor, back inside the cabin, Ishank fought for air, the cloying sweetness of gas stinging his eyes. Ruhi's panicked gasps echoed in his ears, but he knew they couldn't waste energy talking.

"Ruhi, listen close," he rasped, forcing himself to stay calm. "We need to get out of here. Now. He can do anything to Ishita if we don't stop him."

Ruhi, her face pale and streaked with tears, nodded mutely.

They both scrambled for an escape route, their movements frantic as the seconds ticked relentlessly by. A digital clock on the dashboard blinked ominously: 20:00. Twenty minutes left before whatever Anesh had rigged was set to go off. Their eyes darted around the cabin. The windows were boarded shut, thick planks barring their only exit. Despair threatened to engulf Ishank, but a flicker of defiance sparked within him. He wouldn't give up. Not while Ruhi's life hung in the balance.

He spotted a faded curtain hanging limply in one corner. A sliver of hope – maybe there was a window hidden behind it. With a surge of adrenaline, he lunged towards it, ripping the fabric away. Relief flooded him as a small, dusty window peered back at him. It wasn't much, but it was their only chance.

But freedom wasn't so easily attained. The glass was thick and reinforced, designed to withstand the elements, not desperate escape attempts. Time was a cruel adversary. The clock blinked down to 10:00. Panic clawed at Ishank's throat, but he wouldn't give in.

Scanning the room with desperate eyes, his gaze landed on a metal pole holding up a tattered awning. It wasn't ideal, but it would have to do. With a surge of strength fueled by raw terror, he ripped the pole free, its weight straining his already labored muscles.

He swung the makeshift weapon at the window, the metal clanging against the glass with a sickening thud. It held. Time seemed to crawl. Each agonizing clang resonated in the stifling silence of the cabin. 5:00. The air grew thick with the metallic tang of blood as his knuckles split open, but he ignored the pain, his focus solely on shattering their prison.

Finally, with a bone-jarring crack, the glass yielded. A shower of shards rained down, but Ishank barely noticed. He scrambled through the opening, dragging a coughing Ruhi after him. Fresh air, sweet and life-giving, flooded their lungs. They stumbled out of the cabin, collapsing onto the damp grass, gasping for breath.

They lay there, sprawled on the cool earth, the night sky a canvas of a million glittering stars. The taste of freedom was sweeter than anything they'd ever known. But the victory was short-lived. The faint roar of an engine approaching shattered the fragile peace. Through blurry eyes, they saw the headlights of Anesh's car appear on the dusty road, turning a corner and heading straight for them.

"Ruhi," Ishank rasped, clutching his injured side, "get away from here. Hide behind that large crate. This is between me and him. I have to save Ishita. Now go!"

Ruhi obeyed, disappearing behind the crate.

A sudden crack of thunder split the sky, a violent boom that echoed through the emptiness. As if on cue, the heavens opened, unleashing a torrent of rain. The once clear canvas of stars vanished, replaced by an inky blackness. The wind howled, whipping the dust into a frenzy and turning the distant headlights of Anesh's car into blurred, menacing eyes. The storm mirrored the brewing confrontation, a raw and primal energy charged the air, a warning of the coming violence.

Anesh slammed on the brakes, the car lurching forward. He flung himself out of the vehicle, his fists clenched at his sides. He stood there with a steely determination, his eyes fixed on Ishank, as he uttered those chilling words. "How many times, how many times do I have to kill you, my old friend. You always escape death, don't you. But this is your final escape. Let's end this all where it started. But where is your new friend Ruhi."

Ishank, despite his weakened state, mustered the strength to plead with Anesh. "Your fight is with me, Anesh. Please leave Ruhi alone. She has done nothing."

Anesh with a mischievous smile, "Alright, I will deal with her later after finishing you off."

Anesh's face contorted with a mix of rage and determination as he stumbled towards Ishank, who was coughing harshly, his body struggling against the pain. With a fierce grip, Anesh shoved Ishank roughly into the car, his movements fueled by a relentless sense of purpose. Ishita, already bound and silent, sat in the passenger seat, her eyes filled with a mixture of fear and concern for Ishank.

As Anesh took the driver's seat, he cast a glance at Ishank, his eyes burning with a fierce intensity. "You always were the hero, Ishank. Always trying to save everyone. But this time, you won't be able to save yourself."

Ishank, struggling to catch his breath, locked eyes with Anesh, his voice strained but resolute. "Anesh, whatever vendetta you have, it doesn't have to end like this. Let Ishita go. She doesn't deserve to be a pawn in our past."

Anesh's grip tightened on the steering wheel as the car roared to life. Our past, Ishank, is exactly why it must end like this. You ruined everything, and now it's time to pay the price."

Ishita, trembling with fear, attempted to speak, but her muffled voice was barely audible over the hum of the engine. Anesh's gaze flickered to her briefly before returning to the road ahead, a grim determination etched on his face.

The car sped through the winding roads, the tension inside palpable. Anesh's words hung heavy in the air, his eyes fixed on the path ahead as if he were navigating through the memories of their shared past.

Ishank, despite the pain coursing through his body, refused to let fear overtake him. "Anesh, you're not a monster. There's still a chance to make things right. Let's end this madness before it consumes all of us."

Anesh's knuckles whitened as he gripped the steering wheel, his jaw set in a resolute line. "It's too late for second chances, Ishank. You had your opportunities, and you squandered them. Now, we're at the end of the line."

Ishank's gaze flickered to Ishita, silently urging her to stay strong, even as his own strength waned. He knew that they were hurtling towards an unknown fate, one that seemed to grow darker with each passing moment.

Their once carefree laughter was a distant memory, replaced by the suffocating weight of Anesh's twisted obsession. Fueled by a warped sense of justice, Anesh was taking them back to the cliff – the place where he'd nearly ended Ishank's life. This time, though, there would be no turning back.

The car lurched to a halt at the deserted turnoff. Anesh shoved Ishank out, the rain plastering his ragged clothes to his skin. Ishank crumpled to the ground, gasping for breath, the remnants of his previous injuries a stark reminder of Anesh's brutality.

"Looks like you haven't forgotten our little game, have you, Ishank?" Anesh taunted, his voice dripping with venom. "Don't worry, this time it ends for good."

Ishank struggled to his feet, a flicker of defiance igniting in his eyes. "Anesh, this is madness. Don't throw your life away for this." His voice, though weak, held a tremor of desperate hope.

Psychowrath

A cold smile twisted Anesh's lip. "Madness? Maybe. But it's the only way to silence the voices in my head." He lunged forward, grabbing Ishank's injured arm.

Rain hammered down on their entwined forms, blurring vision and slicking the ground into treacherous mud. Ishank and Anesh, once inseparable friends, grappled in a dance of violence that felt more like a grotesque parody of their childhood wrestling matches. Each blow, each desperate scramble for purchase on the slick ground, was a brutal betrayal of their shared past.

Ishank fought with a primal fury born of desperation. Every punch he landed felt heavy with the weight of their shattered bond. Anesh, a mountain of a man fueled by years of festering resentment, fought with a cold efficiency that chilled Ishank to the bone. Yet, in his bloodshot eyes, Ishank saw a flicker of something else – a desperate yearning, a shadow of the friend he once knew.

The fight devolved into a primal struggle, a heartbreaking echo of their childhood brawls. They grappled like wild animals, their laughter replaced by grunts and painful gasps. Ishank, the quicker of the two, used his agility to dodge Anesh's punishing blows. He landed a few himself, each one a searing reminder of the bond they'd broken. A glancing punch split Anesh's lip, a strike that would have elicited a playful shove in their younger days, now drew a roar of feral rage.

But Anesh's strength, fueled by a dark purpose, began to wear Ishank down. Every dodge took more effort, every blow resonated with a dull ache in Ishank's already battered body. He stumbled back, his foot catching a hidden root, and Anesh seized the opportunity. A fist, heavy with the weight of their shattered friendship, connected with Ishank's jaw, sending him sprawling into the mud.

As Ishank lay there, the taste of blood metallic on his tongue, a kaleidoscope of memories flashed before his eyes. Playful sparring sessions in their childhood backyard, whispered secrets under a starlit sky, the shared dreams of their youth, all shattered by a cruel twist of fate. A sob escaped his lips, a sound lost in the howling wind and the relentless drumming of the rain.

Anesh loomed over him, a cruel smile twisting his features. "You see, Ishank," he spat, his voice laced with a venom that poisoned the air, "you can never escape me."

Weakened and drained, Ishank found himself at the mercy of Anesh. He resigned himself to his fate, knowing that his second chance at life was about to end in the same place where it had begun.

But Ishita, despite being bound in the passenger's seat, had other plans.

Rain lashed against the windshield, blurring the already distorted scene playing out before Ishita. Through the blurry haze, she saw Ishank and Anesh locked in a brutal dance. Every punch, every desperate scramble, echoed in her own pounding heart. Panic clawed at her throat.

Her wrists throbbed, a constant reminder of her helplessness. The handcuffs, cold and unforgiving, bit into her skin. But a spark of defiance ignited within her. She wouldn't be a passive observer in her own nightmare. Her gaze darted around the car, searching for anything, anything that could be a weapon, a tool.

Her eyes landed on the rearview mirror. It was a flimsy hope, but it was all she had. With a surge of adrenaline, she twisted in her seat, her back screaming in protest. Using all her remaining strength, she slammed her head against the mirror again and again. Glass rained down on her, a stinging rain that barely registered compared to the urgency that fueled her actions.

Finally, with a sickening crack, the mirror gave way. The shard in her hand wasn't perfect, but it would have to do. Her gaze darted back to her bound wrists. With trembling hands, she sawed at the thin metal of the handcuffs, the jagged edge sending a searing pain through her fingers. Tears welled in her eyes, but she ignored them, focusing on the task at hand.

It felt like an eternity, each scrape against the metal an agonizing tick of the clock. But slowly, painstakingly, a sliver of metal gave way. Then another. Hope, a fragile bud, bloomed in her chest. With a final, desperate push, the handcuff snapped open, falling away from her wrist in a clatter that seemed deafening in the silence of her struggle.

Freedom, a bittersweet sensation, flooded her. But there was no time to celebrate. Her eyes darted to the dashboard, searching for the familiar silhouette of the car key. Relief washed over her as she spotted it dangling from the ignition, a careless oversight by Anesh in his haste.

Reaching across the passenger seat, wincing at the strain it put on her throbbing back, she snatched the key. Her trembling fingers fumbled with the ignition. But finally, with a shudder and a cough, the engine roared to life.

A surge of triumph coursed through her. Gritting her teeth, she slammed her foot on the accelerator.

The car lurched forward, throwing her back against the seat. She fought for control, the steering wheel slick in her rain-soaked hands. The headlights, weak and blurry, barely cut through the downpour, but she focused on the dark silhouette of Anesh in the distance.

With unwavering determination, Ishita steered the car towards Anesh, who stood a distance away from the cliff. Anesh was taken aback by the sudden approach of the car, but before he could react, it was too late. The car hurtled over the cliff's edge, taking both Anesh and Ishita into the depths of darkness.

Ishank, helpless and horrified, could only watch as the tragic scene unfolded before him. A mournful cry escaped his lips, "Ishita." Yet, in the darkness, Ishita's smile lingered in his mind as he closed his eyes. The echo of Ishita's name, a desperate plea swallowed by the hungry maw of the mountain valley, hung heavy in the air long after the car had disappeared. Ishank's world had tilted on its axis.

Grief, a primal and unwelcome guest, took root in his soul. It manifested in a physical ache that radiated from his core, stealing his breath and blurring his vision. He sank to his knees, the dusty floor a poor comfort against the storm raging within him.

Memories, both joyous and sorrowful, flickered through his mind like a silent film. Images of Ishita, her bright smile, the way her eyes crinkled at the corners when she laughed, filled him with a warmth that was quickly extinguished by the memory of her bound form in the car. Her bravery, her unwavering determination to save him, even at the cost of her own life, was a stark contrast to his own perceived cowardice, he thought.

Shame, a searing brand, began to consume him. He berated himself – why hadn't he fought harder? Why hadn't he found a way to stop her from that desperate act? The helplessness he felt, a spectator of the unfolding tragedy, gnawed at him. He had been saved, but at what cost?

Anger, a smoldering ember, flared up amidst the ashes of grief and shame. It wasn't directed at Ishita, her actions fueled by love and a desperate need to protect him. No, his anger was a tempest directed at Anesh, the architect of their misfortune. Years of resentment, the festering wound of betrayal, now ran hot and raw. Anesh, blinded by vengeance, had set in motion a chain of events that had led to this devastating loss.

But the anger, as potent as it was, could not fill the void left by Ishita's absence. She had been the anchor in his life, the beacon of hope that had kept him afloat through the turbulent years since the cellar. Her unwavering belief in him, her gentle strength, allowed him to move forward.

As the initial shock of the incident began to subside, a profound sense of loneliness settled over him. The silence was deafening, broken only by the occasional cough that wracked his weakened body. He was alone, truly alone, adrift in a sea of grief with no shore in sight.

Days bled into nights, the harsh sun and the cold, star-strewn sky offering little solace. He barely slept, haunted by nightmares and the echo of Ishita's scream. He clung to the memories of her, their whispered promises, their shared dreams.

One day, as he sat huddled against a wall, a shaft of sunlight illuminated a small, wilted flower growing through a crack in the floor. The fragile beauty of the blossom struck a chord within him. It was a testament to life's tenacity, its ability to bloom even in the harshest conditions.

The sight of the flower sparked a flicker of determination within him. Ishita wouldn't have wanted him to succumb to despair. He had to honor her memory, to carry forward the spirit of love and resilience she embodied.

Slowly, with the tenacity of the little flower, Ishank began to pull himself together.

Days turned into weeks, weeks into months. The environment, once hostile, began to reveal its secrets. He learned to navigate the treacherous terrain, to read the signs of the weather. He wasn't just surviving, he was adapting.

He wouldn't forget. The past was etched into his soul, a constant reminder of his loss. But with each sunrise, he chose to live, to carry Ishita's memory in his heart. He would find a way to honor her sacrifice, to make her life have meaning.

Chapter Seven: Back From the Dead

Expect the Unexpected

~ Oscar Wilde

When Ishank finally mustered the strength to pull himself together, he decided it was time to visit his parents. The weight of guilt and longing pressed heavily on his chest as he walked down the familiar streets of his childhood neighborhood. It was supposed to bring comfort—a warm embrace of memories. But when he arrived, his heart sank.

The house stood eerily still, its once lively presence now replaced by an overwhelming emptiness. The garden, once meticulously maintained by his father, was now a jungle of weeds and overgrowth. The front door had a faint layer of dust, and the windows looked like hollow eyes staring back at him. He called out, "Mom? Dad?" His voice echoed in the silence, swallowed by the desolation.

It was clear no one had lived here for months. Ishank's mind raced as he stepped inside. The air smelled stale, carrying the unmistakable scent of abandonment. His mother's favorite vase still sat on the mantelpiece, now covered in dust. A photo of the family—taken on a happier day—tilted precariously on the side table. He felt a knot tighten in his stomach.

"Where could they have gone without telling me?" he muttered to himself, panic creeping into his voice.

Desperate for answers, Ishank began searching frantically. First, he combed through the local police stations. He poured over records, flipped through missing persons reports, and even begged an officer to recheck. But there wasn't a single report filed about his parents. Not one. The officers looked at him with pity, offering him advice that sounded hollow.

With no leads and a growing sense of despair, he turned to the only other person he thought might have answers: Ruhi. He raced to her home, the last sliver of hope keeping him going. But as he reached her neighborhood, dread gripped him again. Her house stood locked, its shutters closed tight like secrets refusing to spill.

He knocked hard on the door, his voice cracking as he called out, "Ruhi! Are you in there? It's me, Ishank!" There was no response. Turning to the neighbors, he asked about her family, but their answers made his blood run cold.

"Ruhi and her family? Haven't seen them in months," one of them said, shaking their head.

Frustration bubbled into anger. "Months? How could that be?" Ishank whispered to himself. The despair now felt suffocating, like a hand pressing against his chest. He turned to leave, his mind spiraling into chaos.

But then, out of nowhere, he felt a sudden grip on his wrist. His instincts screamed danger, and he spun around, ready to confront whoever it was.

It was Ruhi.

Her face was pale, her eyes swollen with unshed tears. She looked like she had been running, her breathing shallow and quick.

"Ruhi!" Ishank gasped, relief and confusion colliding within him. He wanted to bombard her with questions, but before he could, she held up her hand.

"Not here," she whispered, her voice trembling. Her eyes darted around the street as if someone—or something—was watching. "Wear this mask and come with me."

Without waiting for a response, Ruhi tugged him along to a small, dimly lit restaurant nearby. They sat in a secluded corner, away from prying eyes. Ishank noticed how her hands trembled as she pushed her hair away from her face.

"Ruhi, what is going on?" Ishank asked, his voice edged with desperation. "Where are my parents? Where is your family? What the hell is happening?"

Tears welled in her eyes, and her lips quivered as she struggled to speak. Finally, she looked him in the eye and said, "Ishank, I think Anesh is back."

The name hit him like a thunderclap. His breath caught in his throat. "What are you saying, Ruhi? That's impossible!"

She leaned closer, her voice barely above a whisper. "He killed your parents, Ishank. Then he came for mine. I… I don't know why I wasn't there to save them." Her voice cracked, and a tear slid down her cheek. "I can't stop seeing their faces in my dreams."

Ishank recoiled, shaking his head. "No, Ruhi. No. That's not possible! I saw him die. I *watched* it with my own eyes! Ishita drove them both over the edge. That car—it went down the cliff. No one could survive that fall."

Ruhi's face darkened, her eyes filled with a mix of fear and certainty. "I thought so too," she said, her voice barely audible. "But I feel it, Ishank. I know it. The demon is back."

The room seemed to shrink around them, the weight of her words filling the air with an almost tangible dread. Outside the restaurant's fogged windows, the city carried on like nothing had happened. But for Ishank and Ruhi, the world as they knew it was unraveling.

A chill ran down Ishank's spine as he whispered, "If Anesh is back… what does he want from us?"

Ruhi's gaze dropped to the table. Her voice was steady now, a grim resolve taking over. "Revenge."

"I don't understand, Ruhi," Ishank said, his voice trembling as though each word carried the weight of his disbelief. "I am so confused. Did you report this to the police? What did they find in their investigation?"

Ruhi's eyes flickered with pain, her hands trembling slightly as she clasped them together. She seemed to stare past him, into a memory too haunting to face head-on.

"Ishank, I reported it the same day my parents went missing," she began, her voice cracking under the strain of reliving the nightmare. "The local police came. They looked around, asked questions, scribbled in their little notebooks, but... nothing. They found nothing. A few weeks later, they told me they'd done everything they could."

Her breath hitched, and she closed her eyes tightly, as if trying to push back the tears threatening to spill. "They said my parents were probably dead. That there was no hope. I was completely shattered." Her voice wavered, and she paused, swallowing hard before continuing.

"I didn't know what to do. I went to your house looking for help, but it was empty. No one was there. That's when it hit me." Her gaze locked onto his, raw and piercing. "It had to be Anesh. He's the only one capable of this kind of cruelty. I knew I had to disappear before he turned his attention to me. I've been living in constant fear, Ishank. And the worst part? I thought he'd already killed you."

Her words hung in the air, heavy and bitter. Ishank leaned forward, his heart aching at the sight of her fragility. He reached out, his fingers brushing against hers in a quiet gesture of comfort.

"I'm sorry, Ruhi," he whispered, his voice barely audible. "I don't know what you've been through. But I swear, we'll make this right."

For a moment, neither of them spoke. The silence was broken only by the faint chirping of crickets outside and the distant murmur of city life. Then Ruhi looked at him, her expression softening, a glimmer of hope peeking through her fear. "Where have you been all these months?"

Ishank's jaw tightened, and his gaze drifted to the floor. "I don't even know, Ruhi," he admitted, his voice heavy with guilt. "After I saw Ishita... die, right in front of me, I lost myself. Completely. I wandered, aimless, broken. But that's another story. Right now, we need to focus on our parents." His eyes sharpened, the fire of determination rekindled within him. "Don't lose hope. If Anesh is still out there, he won't let our parents die so easily. This isn't over, Ruhi. Not by a long shot. He's planning something. I can feel it."

Ruhi shook her head, doubt clouding her features. "Ishank, I've tried everything. Every lead, every clue... it's like they vanished into thin air. Where would we even start?"

The shadow of a smile ghosted across Ishank's lips, but it wasn't one of humor. It was grim, resolute. He leaned closer, his voice dropping to a conspiratorial whisper. "I know where to find him."

Ruhi's eyes widened, the flicker of hope growing brighter. "You do?"

"Yes," he replied, his tone unyielding. "But we'll need to be careful. He isn't just playing games. He's setting a trap, and we're walking straight into it."

Outside, a dog barked in the distance, its sound sharp against the stillness of the night. The faint rustling of leaves added an ominous undertone to the charged atmosphere in the room. Ruhi and Ishank exchanged a look—a silent pact forged in the crucible of their shared pain.

For the first time in months, Ruhi felt something stir within her: the faint, flickering flame of hope.

The crisp night air outside the restaurant seemed to hold a faint promise of normalcy as Ishank and Ruhi stepped out, their footsteps echoing on the empty sidewalk. The gentle hum of passing traffic was the only sound until it wasn't.

From the shadows, men clad in dark clothes and a woman in a hood emerged swiftly, their movements calculated and precise. Before Ishank and Ruhi could react, rough hands seized them. Masks were shoved over their heads, their protests muffled and futile as they struggled against the iron grip of their captors.

"Let us go!" Ishank growled, thrashing in vain.

Ruhi's muffled cries pierced the chaos. "What is happening? Stop this!"

Their resistance was short-lived. Overpowered and blindfolded, they were shoved into the back of a vehicle. The engine roared to life, and the car sped off into the night.

The journey felt endless, every twist and turn of the car adding to their disorientation. The air inside the vehicle was tense, filled with an eerie silence broken only by the occasional muffled whisper of their captors.

After what seemed like an eternity—more than an hour later—they were unceremoniously dragged out of the car and led down a series of steps. When the masks were finally yanked off their heads, Ishank and Ruhi blinked rapidly, their eyes adjusting to the dim fluorescent lighting.

They were in a basement. The air was heavy with the faint hum of machinery and the clicking of keyboards. Computers lined the walls, their screens glowing with streams of data. Officers in plain clothes moved with quiet efficiency, focused on their tasks. The atmosphere buzzed with an urgency that suggested this was no ordinary facility.

Ruhi clutched Ishank's arm, her voice barely above a whisper. "What is this place?"

Ishank, still disoriented, shouted, "Where are we? What is going on? Can somebody tell us what this is?"

As if on cue, a young officer stepped forward. His sharp, determined features were illuminated by the light from a nearby monitor. He carried himself with a confidence that suggested he was used to taking charge.

"Hello, Ishank and Ruhi," he began, his tone calm but firm. "I am Ronak, the head of this special unit. Welcome to the Special Crimes Unit, or SCU. I apologize for the way we brought you here, but it was necessary. Trust me, you're safe now. We're all fighting the same enemy."

Ruhi's brows furrowed. "How do you even know about us?" she asked, her voice laced with both suspicion and curiosity.

Ronak's expression darkened. "Mr. Kapoor," he said quietly, "was a dear friend of mine. We grew up together. When he was brutally murdered by Anesh, it shattered me. It was more than personal—it became my mission. Then, I heard about the disappearance of your parents." He paused, his fists clenching at his sides. "I swore I'd take down that demon, Anesh, with my own hands."

Ishank's jaw tightened, his voice cutting through the room like a blade. "But Anesh is dead! He died the day Mr. Kapoor was killed. I saw it with my own eyes. Are you telling me my own eyes lied to me?"

Ronak's gaze met Ishank's, unyielding. "I don't care what you saw, Ishank. He's alive. And this time, he won't escape. We're going to end this once and for all."

The tension in the room was palpable, the air crackling with the weight of their shared pain and anger.

Ronak gestured for them to follow. "Come with me. There's something you need to see."

They followed him through a narrow corridor into a small room dominated by a large screen. Ronak pressed a few keys, and grainy footage began to play.

"This was captured near Ruhi's house, days before your parents went missing," Ronak explained.

On the screen, a man in his late 40s moved through the shadows. His face was obscured by the poor quality of the camera, but his behavior was unmistakably suspicious. He seemed to be inspecting the area, his movements calculated and deliberate.

"This man," Ronak continued, "was seen loitering near your house. We believe he was gathering information, figuring out when your parents would be most vulnerable. This footage confirms that Anesh isn't acting alone. He has people working with him."

Ruhi's breath hitched. "But… who is he? Why would anyone help Anesh?"

Ronak's eyes hardened. "That's what we're trying to find out. But make no mistake—whoever this is, they're just as dangerous as Anesh himself. We're close, Ishank and Ruhi. Closer than ever."

The room fell silent, the faint hum of the monitor filling the void. Ishank and Ruhi exchanged a look, their fear mingling with a renewed determination. The battle wasn't over. It was just beginning.

The night was cold, with a faint mist clinging to the hills as the group sat huddled in their car parked at the edge of the winding road leading to Anesh's ancestral home in Kasauli. The silhouette of the house loomed against the starless sky, its dark windows like watchful eyes. The air was heavy with tension as Ishank spoke, breaking the silence.

"Sir," Ishank began, his voice steady despite the nervous energy crackling in the car. "We should start at Anesh's home. If he's alive, he might've left something behind, or perhaps he visited his parents. We might find a clue there."

Ronak nodded thoughtfully, his eyes fixed on the shadowy outline of the house. "You're right, Ishank. But this time, we need to plan carefully. Anesh has proven he's always one step ahead. We can't afford any mistakes."

The plan was simple but precise: they would approach the house at dawn, under the cover of daylight but with utmost caution.

The next morning, the group set out—Ronak, Ishank, Ruhi, and two officers, their black SUV winding through the sleepy streets of Kasauli. The chilly mountain air nipped at their faces as they parked a short distance from the house.

Ronak turned to Ishank and Ruhi, his expression firm. "Ishank, you and Ruhi stay here. There's no telling what dangers might be inside. We'll go in and be back as soon as possible."

Ishank hesitated but nodded. "Understood, sir. We'll wait here. Be careful."

As Ronak and his two officers stepped out, their boots crunching softly against the gravel, the tension in the air seemed to thicken. The officers gripped their firearms tightly, their eyes scanning every corner as they approached the house.

The once-pristine colonial-style home now looked forlorn, its paint peeling and its garden overrun with weeds. The wind whispered through broken shutters, adding an eerie undertone to the already charged atmosphere.

They moved cautiously, their guns raised, until they reached the overgrown garden at the back of the house. There, seated in an old chair, was their man, Anesh's father.

Ronak raised his hand, signaling his team to lower their weapons. "Stand down," he murmured, stepping forward.

The man looked up, his voice hoarse as he spat out, "Police? What do you want now? That monster who was born in this house is already gone. What could you possibly want?"

Ronak's voice was calm but firm. "Sir, we're not here to harm you. We need your help. Your son, Anesh, is alive. He has kidnapped Ruhi and Ishank's parents. Please, tell us anything you know. Have you noticed anything unusual since his supposed death?"

Anesh's father let out a bitter laugh, the sound dry and hollow. "Alive, is he? Well, I don't care. I've mourned the loss of my son long before you came here. The man you speak of isn't my son anymore. He died the day he became a monster."

Ronak studied the man's face carefully. "Do you mind if we take a look around your house? We won't disturb anything."

 "Go ahead. But don't move anything. My better half isn't here to keep things in order anymore, and I can't find things as easily as she did." said his father.

Inside, the house was an odd mix of neglect and care. Dust clung to the furniture, but one room stood out starkly—a room filled with trophies, medals, and certificates. Ronak entered cautiously, taking in the well-organized shelves. Every trophy gleamed, spotless, as though polished regularly.

Ronak's brow furrowed as he inspected the room. It seemed untouched by time, as if frozen in the memory of a boy who excelled in studies and sports. The contrast between the room's pristine state and the rest of the house felt unnerving.

He muttered under his breath, "How could someone so accomplished turn into a killer?"

As if sensing his thoughts, Anesh's father appeared in the doorway. "You're wondering about the room, aren't you?"

Ronak turned, startled. "It's… unusually well-kept."

The man sighed, his voice heavy with grief. "This was my son before he became what you call a monster. A bright boy, full of promise. I clean this room because it's the only part of him I can still love. The boy who loved his parents. Not the man who destroyed lives."

Ronak nodded, his tone softening. "I understand. Thank you for letting us look around. If you come across anything—anything at all—please don't hesitate to call me." He handed over his card.

The man took it without a word. As Ronak turned to leave, he heard the man murmur under his breath, "The dead never rise again."

Ronak stopped and looked back. "Did you say something?"

The man straightened, his face carefully blank. "No. I'll let you know if I see anything."

Ronak studied him for a moment longer, then nodded. "Thank you."

As Ronak and his team left the house, the weight of the encounter lingered. The air outside felt colder, heavier, as if the house itself carried the burden of its dark history.

Back in the car, Ishank and Ruhi waited anxiously. "Did you find anything?" Ishank asked as Ronak slid into the passenger seat.

"Not yet," Ronak said, his tone measured. "But something about that house isn't right. We'll find him, Ishank. We're getting closer."

Ronak gripped the steering wheel tightly, his mind churning with Anesh's father's haunting words: *"The dead never rise again."* The weight of those words hung in the air like a storm cloud, adding to the tension crackling between them.

Ruhi broke the silence, her voice tentative but filled with urgency. "What do we do next?"

Ishank leaned forward, his eyes glinting with determination. "Ronak sir, I think we should check my house. It might hold something—anything—that could lead us forward."

Ronak nodded. "You read my mind, Ishank. Your house is only a few doors away. Let's check it out."

The group arrived at Ishank's family home, the familiar yet eerie silhouette of the house looming in the dim moonlight. The front door creaked ominously as they stepped in, the air heavy with the scent of dust and neglect.

Ishank stepped forward instinctively. "This is my home. I know every corner of it. Let me help you search."

Ronak held up a hand, firm but understanding. "I might need your help, but don't touch anything. We'll need the fingerprints for analysis. Ruhi," he added, turning to her, "stay outside with one of my officers. We'll call you if we find something."

Ruhi hesitated but nodded, her expression uneasy. Ronak instructed one of the officers, Karan, to stay with her as they entered the house.

Inside, the house felt like a time capsule, frozen in the moment before tragedy struck. Dust motes danced in the faint light streaming through cracked windows. Photographs hung crooked on the walls, and the air carried a faint metallic tang of dried blood.

Ronak, Ishank, and an officer moved methodically through the house. Every corner, every crevice was scrutinized. Ishank's eyes darted around, his face a mixture of nostalgia and dread.

"Sir," Ishank called out, his voice trembling as he pointed to the floor near the living room. "This is my father's watch. I gave it to him on his birthday."

Ronak crouched down, pulling on a fresh pair of gloves before carefully picking up the watch. He examined it briefly before placing it into an evidence bag held out by the officer.

They moved toward the bedroom, the carpeted floor faintly marked with overlapping footprints. Ronak crouched to inspect them. "Two sets of prints," he observed, his tone clinical but focused. "One belongs to your father. The other… likely the intruder."

The trio pressed onward, entering the kitchen. It was eerily pristine except for a dark stain on the tiled floor. Ronak's sharp gaze zeroed in on the faint blood spatter near the countertop.

"The kidnapper was smart," Ronak muttered, tracing the outline of the stain with his gloved finger. "He likely struck your mother here first with a blunt object. The blow didn't kill her—just enough to knock her unconscious. He then moved to the bedroom to deal with your father. No blood there, which means he disabled him with minimal violence, just enough to overpower him."

Ishank's jaw tightened, his fists clenched at his sides.

Ronak stood and exhaled sharply. "We've got enough evidence to analyze for now. Let's regroup and—"

A piercing scream shattered the silence.

"Ruhi!" Ishank bolted toward the sound, his heart pounding as Ronak and the officer followed close behind.

They burst through the front door to find chaos. The officer who had been guarding Ruhi lay crumpled near the car, groaning in pain. Ruhi was nowhere to be seen.

Ronak dropped to his knees beside the injured officer, gripping his shoulders. "What happened? Where is Ruhi? Who was here?" His voice was sharp, barely masking the rising panic.

The officer winced, blood trickling from the back of his head. "I… I don't know, sir. Someone attacked me from behind. It happened so fast. I didn't see their face. They took her… and vanished."

Ronak's face hardened, his jaw tightening. "They couldn't have gone far. Ishank, with me."

Ronak and Ishank sprinted into the darkness, their breaths coming in ragged gasps. The cold night air bit at their skin as they searched the surrounding streets and alleys. Every shadow seemed to mock their desperation, every corner they turned yielding nothing but emptiness.

After what felt like an eternity, they returned to the car, their failure weighing heavily on them. Ishank's face was a mask of fury and grief, his knuckles white as he clenched his fists.

Ronak placed a hand on his shoulder, his voice steady despite the turmoil inside him. "We'll find her, Ishank. I promise you. But right now, we need to regroup and think this through. Losing our focus won't help her."

Ishank's shoulders sagged, his anger giving way to despair. "She's out there, with *them*. We can't let them take her, Ronak."

"We won't," Ronak said firmly, his eyes narrowing. "This isn't over. Not by a long shot."

Chapter Eight: One Last Time

Everything Depends On Upbringing

~Leo Tolstoy

Ronak's SUV screeched to a halt in front of the Special Crimes Unit (SCU). The atmosphere inside the facility was thick with urgency, the hum of computers and the rapid clicking of keyboards filling the air as officers worked tirelessly on various cases. The team moved quickly, their faces reflecting the gravity of the situation.

Ronak handed over the evidence bag containing the fingerprints he had collected from Ishank's house to one of the forensic officers. "Run these through the database," he instructed, his voice sharp and commanding. "We need to know who these belong to. Prioritize this immediately."

As the officer hurried away, Ronak turned to another team member stationed at a computer. "Trace Ruhi's mobile phone," he ordered.

The officer's fingers flew across the keyboard, the screen flickering with data streams and location coordinates. After a few tense moments, he looked up, his expression grim. "Sir, her phone is dead. No signal, no last location."

Ronak's face tightened, his usual composure slipping for just a moment. He muttered under his breath, "There has to be something—one clue, one lead—and I'll drag that monster out of whatever hole he's hiding in."

Just then, a female officer called out from across the room, her voice cutting through the tense air. "Sir, I've compared the fingerprints you brought with those of Anesh. They don't match."

Ronak and Ishank approached her desk, both visibly unsettled. Ishank's brows furrowed deeply. "Does that mean… Anesh really is dead? Was I right all along?"

Ronak's jaw clenched as he considered the implications. "If these prints aren't Anesh's, then our suspicions shift elsewhere…" His voice trailed off as he reached into his pocket, pulling out a small case containing an old medal.

He handed it to the female officer. "Run a comparison with the prints on this medal. If I'm right, we're closer than we think."

As the officer took the medal and began her analysis, Ishank turned to Ronak, his voice heavy with frustration and desperation. "Sir, who are we even looking for now? And how will we find Ruhi if her phone's dead?"

Ronak placed a firm hand on Ishank's shoulder, his eyes meeting Ishank's with steely resolve. "Ishank, listen to me. Don't lose hope. If my suspicion is correct, we're dealing with someone we've overlooked—someone who's been operating in the shadows all along."

The officer at the computer suddenly straightened, her voice cutting through the room like a knife. "Ronak sir, the fingerprints match."

Ronak's head snapped toward her. "Who are they from?"

The officer turned the screen to face him, her voice steady but tinged with disbelief. "They match… 99.9%. The fingerprints belong to—"

The sterile light of the investigation room flickered slightly, casting long shadows on the walls as Ronak leaned over the fingerprint scanner. The room buzzed with quiet intensity—officers typing on keyboards, a faint hum of computers filling the air. Ronak stared at the results on the screen, his brow furrowing deeper.

"These fingerprints," he said, his voice heavy, "are of Anesh's father, Ishank. This changes everything."

Ishank's breath hitched as he processed the revelation. "Anesh's father?" he echoed, his voice low and filled with disbelief. "But… why? What does he have to do with all this?"

Ronak straightened, his face grim. "Now I understand the cause behind Anesh's twisted upbringing. Anesh didn't fall into darkness—he was raised in it."

Before Ishank could respond, a young officer's voice cut through the room, sharp and urgent. "Sir, we've received a video from an unknown source."

Ronak's gaze snapped toward him. "Play it," he ordered, his voice cold and commanding.

The room fell silent as the lights dimmed, and the large screen in front of them lit up. The video began static, then slowly came into focus. The face that appeared sent a chill down Ishank's spine—a gaunt, menacing figure with hollow eyes and a malicious smirk.

"Ronak Boss," the man said, his voice dripping with mockery and malice, "you've probably figured it out by now. Yes, it's me. The puppet master behind everything. From kidnapping Ishank's parents to taking Ruhi's parents. And now, I've added Ruhi to my little collection. Surprised?"

The man leaned closer to the camera, his face filling the screen. His expression darkened, the smirk turning into something more sinister. "I'm sure you're dying to know why, aren't you? Well, let's make it simple. Ishank killed my son, Anesh. And you see, Ronak, I believe in Karma. It's time for payback."

Ishank clenched his fists, his knuckles turning white. "That monster," he hissed under his breath.

Ronak placed a calming hand on his shoulder but didn't take his eyes off the screen.

Anesh's father continued, his voice rising with theatrical flair. "But I'm not an unreasonable man. No, no. I'm actually quite… merciful. I'm giving you a chance, Ishank."

He paused, leaning back as though savoring the moment. "Let's play a little game. You took my son's life, and now it's your turn to choose whose life will pay the price. Will it be one of your dear parents? Or perhaps someone from Ruhi's family?"

The room was deathly silent, save for the soft whirring of the video. Ishank's heart pounded in his chest, each word tightening the noose around him.

The man's smirk grew wider. "Oh, and if you're thinking of refusing to choose—if you're hoping to play the noble hero—let me tell you what happens then. I'll take them all. Every. Single. One. You have 36 hours, Ishank. Your time starts… now."

The screen momentarily flickered, but then the man leaned forward again, his face filling the frame once more. His eyes burned with malice. "And did I mention? I'm far, far away. So don't even think about trying to find me. You'd only be wasting time. Tick-tock, Ishank. Tick-tock."

With that, the screen went black, leaving the room plunged into an oppressive silence.

Ishank's breathing was ragged as he struggled to process the sheer weight of the threat.

Ronak's voice was steady but sharp. "Stay calm, Ishank. Losing your head won't help her—or your parents." He turned to his team. "Track the source of that video. I don't care if he claims he's far away—there's always a trail. Find it."

The officers nodded and sprang into action, their keyboards clacking furiously as they dove into the task.

Ishank turned to Ronak, his eyes blazing. "We can't just wait around. He gave us 36 hours. What if they're already…" His voice cracked, unable to finish the thought.

Ronak placed both hands on Ishank's shoulders, meeting his gaze with unwavering intensity. "We're going to find him. And we're going to stop him. But we need to think smart. This isn't just a kidnapping—it's a carefully orchestrated game. Every move he makes is calculated. If we're not careful, he'll win."

"I can't lose them, Ronak," Ishank whispered, his voice breaking. "Not again."

"You won't," Ronak promised. "But we need to move quickly. His arrogance will be his downfall. He left us a breadcrumb trail—we just need to follow it."

The room buzzed with activity as officers worked to trace the video's origin. The tension was palpable, every second stretching into an eternity.

As Ronak watched his team, his mind raced through the possibilities. Anesh's father had shown his hand, but Ronak knew there was more to this game than met the eye. And if they were going to win, they needed to be one step ahead.

"We're coming for you," Ronak muttered under his breath, his jaw tightening. "And this time, you won't get away."

He stood at the center of the makeshift command station, his sharp eyes scanning the faces of his team.

He pointed decisively at two of his officers, his voice calm but commanding.

"You two," he said, his tone leaving no room for argument, "head to Anesh's house. There's something about that place… something it's hiding. I don't care how mundane it looks; investigate every corner, every crack in the walls. Look for anything—scratches, hidden compartments, misplaced furniture. Don't ignore a single detail. And for God's sake, be careful."

The officers exchanged quick glances and snapped to attention. "Roger that, sir!" they chorused before grabbing their gear and heading out into the night.

As the sound of their departure faded, Ronak turned back to the dimly lit screen in front of him. The video file, grainy and distorted, was paused at a frame. Ronak leaned closer, his sharp features illuminated by the cold glow of the monitor.

"Play it again," he instructed, his voice quieter now but no less authoritative.

The officer at the computer nodded and hit the play button. The video began to roll, the faint flicker of motion drawing everyone's attention. Ronak's eyes narrowed, his mind racing to dissect every detail.

"Pause," he ordered abruptly, and the video froze mid-frame. "Give me the headphones," he added, holding out his hand.

The officer quickly handed them over. Ronak adjusted them over his ears, his brow furrowing in concentration as he replayed the clip, this time focusing on the audio. He closed his eyes, blocking out the distractions around him, and listened intently.

There it was—a faint symphony of sounds beneath the static. The soft rustling of leaves, the gentle chirping of birds, and a distant hum that could have been flowing water. Ronak opened his eyes and pulled the headphones off with a sharp breath.

"He's not in a city," Ronak said, his voice filled with quiet certainty. "There's no traffic noise, no urban clatter. The background is too clean. I can hear birds chirping—distinctly. He's in a quiet place. A village, maybe. Or somewhere in the mountains. Somewhere remote where the world doesn't drown out nature."

Ronak turned to Ishank, his gaze piercing. "And if we follow the trail, it leads us back near his old house. He wouldn't abandon familiar ground completely. That house isn't just a memory—it's a connection, a tether to his past. He'd want to be close to it, but far enough to avoid suspicion."

Ishank's fists clenched, his knuckles white. "Then that's where we need to focus. Near Anesh's house. He's there, I'm sure of it. And if he's there, so are the answers we're looking for."

Ronak's lips curved into a thin, grim smile. "He may have been a step ahead so far, but the final move is ours to make. We won't just find him, Ishank—we'll bring him down."

The officer manning the computer interrupted, his voice hesitant. "Sir, I've enhanced the video as much as I can. There's a faint reflection in the window behind him—a tree line, maybe. It's not much, but it looks like conifers. Could be the hills."

Ronak nodded approvingly. "Good work. Keep analyzing that footage. Any detail, no matter how small, could break this case wide open."

Meanwhile, Ishank's mind raced, his thoughts a chaotic jumble of memories, possibilities, and raw emotion. "Ronak sir," he said hesitantly, "what if he knows we're onto him? What if this is a trap?"

Ronak's face hardened. "Then we spring it. But not on his terms—on ours. Anesh's father is still out there, he's desperate. And desperation makes people reckless. That's when they make mistakes."

The room fell into a tense silence as everyone absorbed Ronak's words. The officers dispatched to Anesh's house had yet to report back, and the air felt thick with anticipation. Somewhere out there, the elusive mastermind they were hunting was lying in wait.

Ronak walked to the window and looked out into the night, the moonlight casting sharp shadows across his face. "He thinks he's untouchable," he murmured, more to himself than anyone else. "But arrogance is his weakness. He left traces, and now we'll follow them to wherever he's hiding."

Ishank stepped beside him, his voice firm. "And when we find him?"

Ronak turned to face him, his eyes blazing with resolve. "When we find him, Ishank… we end this."

Ronak and Ishank moved stealthily through the dimly lit streets, their hearts pounding with urgency. The air was thick with tension as they approached Anesh's father's house, a seemingly innocuous structure that concealed dark secrets.

"I'm convinced he's hiding somewhere in his own home," Ronak said, glancing at Ishank, whose brow was furrowed with worry. "A basement, a secret room—he has to be here. The footage we saw looked eerily familiar. We need to find him before he makes his next move." His voice was steady, but the underlying fear was palpable.

Ishank nodded, determination etched on his face despite the anxiety swirling within him. They stepped inside the house, the creaking floorboards echoing their every move. Dust motes danced in the shafts of moonlight filtering through grimy windows. They began their search methodically, rummaging through drawers and closets, pulling apart furniture as if it were a puzzle waiting to be solved.

Suddenly, Ishank's phone buzzed violently in his pocket, shattering the silence like a gunshot. He pulled it out, his hands trembling as he read the notification. "Another video!" he exclaimed, his voice taut with tension.

"Open it! Come on, fast!" Ronak urged, his eyes wide with urgency.

With shaking fingers, Ishank tapped the screen. The video flickered to life, revealing Anesh's father, his expression a twisted mask of malice and glee. "Still searching in my house?" he taunted, his voice dripping with mockery. "Time's running out, Ishank. Just 24 hours left before you'll never find me in this life again. Make your choices quickly."

Ishank felt a chill run down his spine as the man continued, "And speaking of choices... I suddenly remember that I'll take two lives because you not only killed my son but my grandchild too! Ishita was pregnant, Ishank—she had Anesh's baby in her womb. How unfortunate that I never got to see my unborn grandchild."

The weight of those words hung heavy in the air, suffocating Ishank as he processed the implications of what was being said.

"Past is past," Anesh's father continued with an unsettling calmness. "Let's move on to the future now. I'm getting a little bored with this game, so here's my offer: I will kill one of your loved ones in about ten hours. Make your choice fast or it could be anyone of them that I may kill. Tada!"

The video cut off abruptly, leaving an oppressive silence in its wake. Tears streamed down Ishank's cheeks as he whispered hoarsely, "Ishika was pregnant."

Ronak placed a firm hand on Ishank's shoulder, trying to ground him in this moment of despair. "But she had Anesh's child," he replied gently but firmly. "You need to calm down."

"It doesn't matter!" Ishank shouted, his voice cracking under the weight of emotion. "I loved her! I would've accepted her child without hesitation!"

Ronak took a deep breath, trying to maintain control over the spiraling situation. "Ishank," he said softly but with authority, "the past is gone now. We have to focus on what lies ahead of us." He paused for a moment before continuing with conviction. "This was a bluff—he wants us here wasting time while he plots his next move. He's playing us like pawns in a game."

The room felt colder as they stood amidst the chaos they had created during their search—a stark contrast to the warmth of memories that haunted Ishank's mind. The walls seemed to close in around them as Ronak scanned their surroundings for any clues that might lead them closer to Anesh's father but they found nothing.

Ishank wiped his tears away; they had no time to waste on grief now.

"Ishank," Ronak said, his voice steady but urgent, "send that video to my phone. I'll have it checked by my team. Maybe they can dig up some clues."

With a nod, Ishank quickly sent the video, his fingers trembling slightly as he pressed 'send.' Ronak's heart raced as he forwarded it to his team, a flicker of hope igniting within him.

He took a deep breath and dialed a number, the ringing tone echoing in the stillness of the hills. When the line connected, he spoke briskly, "I've sent you a video. Check it thoroughly for any clues. Also, circulate Anesh's father's picture across the city—see if anyone recognizes him. We're running out of time, and he's becoming more dangerous by the minute. Oh, and track the number of the sender."

As he hung up, a sense of urgency enveloped them. The hills were eerily quiet except for the rustling leaves and distant calls of birds settling in for the night. Time slipped away like sand through their fingers as they combed through every crevice and shadow.

Hours passed—nine to be exact—when Ronak's phone buzzed sharply in his pocket. He answered it with bated breath but soon felt his heart sink as he cut the call.

"They tried tracing the number," he told Ishank, frustration lacing his words. "But they found nothing. He knows how to play these tech tricks."

Just then, Ishank's phone vibrated violently against his thigh, breaking the tense silence. He glanced at it and frowned; a link to a video call flashed ominously on his screen from an untraceable website.

"What now?" Ronak asked, dread pooling in his stomach.

"I don't know," Ishank replied hesitantly but clicked on it anyway. The screen flickered to life, revealing Anesh's father—a figure cloaked in shadows yet radiating menace.

"Nine hours gone, Ishank beta, *"Anesh's father taunted, a sinister smile playing on his lips.* "And I think you're still struggling to figure out whose life I should take. Any progress?"

Ishank felt a cold sweat break out across his forehead as panic surged through him. "Please," he pleaded desperately, "for God's sake, leave them all alone! I'm your culprit; kill me instead! I'm ready to do whatever you tell me."

Anesh's father chuckled darkly, his eyes glinting with malice. "You know, Ishank," he said slowly, savoring each word like fine wine, "you should feel what it's like when your loved one is gone—that is your fate now. Tell me quickly who to kill; otherwise, I'll have to make my own move."

The air thickened with tension as Ishank's heart raced uncontrollably. He felt trapped in a nightmare from which there was no escape.

"Okay…" His voice trembled as he forced himself to speak the words that felt like daggers piercing through him. "Kill my father."

Those words hung in the air like a death sentence—a heavy silence enveloping them both as if time itself had paused in disbelief.

Anesh's father leaned closer to the screen, an unsettling grin spreading across his face. "I knew you would sacrifice your dear old dad,*" he said gleefully.* "That's why I've already made arrangements for him."

Ishank's stomach twisted painfully as dread washed over him.

"He will be breathing his last breath in this little cabin we call Earth.*" The man leaned back in his chair with an air of triumph.* "Goodbye Ishank; get ready for your final choice in just fourteen hours."

As the call ended abruptly with a click that echoed like a gunshot in Ishank's ears, he felt the world around him crumble into chaos—his heart pounding like a war drum against his ribcage.

Ronak placed a comforting hand on Ishank's shoulder but could find no words to ease the turmoil brewing within him. They stood together under the fading light of day—both caught in a web of desperation and fear—with only time slipping away between them and an impending tragedy that threatened to tear their lives apart forever.

The air was thick with tension as Ishank leaned forward, his eyes wide with urgency. "Sir, what did he just say in the call about the cabin... and breathing?" His voice trembled slightly, a mix of fear and determination.

Ronak, his mentor and a seasoned detective, glanced at Ishank, his brow furrowed in thought. "Yes, he said that *your father will be breathing his last breath in this little cabin we call Earth.*" The weight of those words hung heavily between them, a grim reminder of the race against time they faced.

Ishank's heart raced as he processed the chilling message. "I know where my father is!" he exclaimed suddenly, springing from his chair as if propelled by an unseen force. The urgency in his voice cut through the tension like a knife.

"Where, Ishank? Tell me! We need to go there now!" Ronak urged, his own pulse quickening at the prospect of saving Ishank's father.

"Anesh once trapped us in his house where he lived with Ishita," Ishank replied, his voice shaking with the memory. "He left Ruhi and me to die in that cabin of his house with some poisonous gas. We barely escaped." The recollection of that harrowing day flashed across his mind—darkness creeping in, the suffocating air, and the feeling of hopelessness.

Ronak's expression hardened. "How much time does it take to reach there?"

"Forty to forty-five minutes if we drive fast," Ishank responded, determination igniting within him.

"Let's go then!" Ronak said decisively, already moving toward the door.

They rushed to the car, adrenaline surging through their veins. Ronak gripped the steering wheel tightly as he accelerated down the road.

As they sped along, Ishank felt a storm of emotions swirling within him—fear for his father's life, anger at Anesh's father for putting them in this situation, and a flicker of hope that they could still save him. "We have to make it in time," he muttered under his breath.

After what felt like an eternity, Ronak pulled into the gravel driveway leading up to the cabin. The old structure loomed ahead, its weathered wood and peeling paint telling stories of neglect and despair. They had just ten minutes left before the gas would engulf the house completely.

"Come on!" Ronak shouted as they leapt from the car, urgency propelling them forward. They dashed toward the door but found it locked tight. Panic surged through Ishank as he rattled the handle futilely.

"Let me deal with it, sir," he said breathlessly. He stepped back for a moment and then charged at the door with all his might. With a loud crash, it splintered open, revealing a dimly lit interior filled with shadows that danced ominously along the walls.

"Dad!" Ishank called out desperately as they entered. The stench of stale air mixed with something far more sinister filled their lungs. Time was slipping away like sand through their fingers.

They moved quickly through the cramped space—a living room cluttered with old furniture and remnants of a life once lived. "This way!" Ronak shouted, leading Ishank toward a closed door at the end of a narrow hallway.

With each step, dread coiled tighter around Ishank's heart. What if they were too late? What if they opened that door only to find... nothing?

Ronak kicked open the door with force; it swung wide to reveal a cabin where Ishank's father lay unconscious on the floor. His face was pale as death itself; beads of sweat glistened on his forehead.

"No! Dad!" Ishank rushed forward, kneeling beside him. He could feel panic rising within him like bile. "Please wake up!"

Ronak quickly checked for signs of life while Ishank cradled his father's head in his lap. "He's still breathing," Ronak said urgently but calmly. "We need to get him out of here—now!"

With great effort, they lifted Ishank's father together, their muscles straining against the weight of despair that threatened to crush them both. As they stumbled back through the house, Ronak glanced at Ishank. "Keep talking to him! Your voice will help him stay conscious."

"Dad! Please stay with me!" Ishank pleaded as they reached the front door just as a faint hissing sound began to fill the air behind them—the gas was seeping in.

They burst out into the cool night air just moments before darkness threatened to swallow them whole. Ronak rushed them to the car while Ishank held his father tightly against him.

"Drive! Drive!" Ishank shouted as Ronak jumped into the driver's seat and started the engine with trembling hands.

As they sped away from that cursed cabin, relief washed over Ishank like a tide pulling back from shore—but it was mixed with an overwhelming sense of dread for what lay ahead. They had saved his father this time—but still four lives were on the stake.

After admitting Ishank's father to the hospital, Ronak and Ishank returned to the Special Crimes Unit (SCU), the weight of the world pressing down on their shoulders. The sterile scent of antiseptic filled the air, a stark contrast to the chaos swirling in their minds. Ronak, a seasoned detective with a steely resolve, deployed two of his officers at the hospital, ensuring that Ishank's father would be guarded during this precarious time.

Five hours remained, and just as the clock ticked ominously, a message flashed on Ishank's mobile phone. His heart raced as he read the chilling words:

"Ishank the savior, you may have saved your father and I should congratulate you on that. But you know I don't like to negotiate things with my counterparts. Two lives are at stake and 5 hours to go. I will ask you about your next two choices in 4 hours."

The message sent a shiver down Ishank's spine. He felt a mix of dread and determination wash over him.

Ronak clenched his jaw, his voice steady yet laced with urgency. "We have no clue about what he's going to do next, but we must do our best to save them. I don't want any bloodshed at all. He wants to play a game? Let's play it on our terms." His confidence was palpable, a beacon of hope in the storm.

"What do you mean, sir?" Ishank asked, his brow furrowed with confusion and fear.

"What I mean, Ishank, is that Anesh's father is some kind of maniac, just like Anesh himself. In cases like these, there's always a pattern; we just need to follow it and unleash our strategy when we have the chance." Ronak's eyes glinted with determination as he strode toward a board cluttered with case details pinned haphazardly with red strings crisscrossing between them.

He began to piece together the puzzle before him, snapping pictures and jotting down notes with a fervor that ignited Ishank's own resolve.

"Here," Ronak pointed emphatically at one particular section of the board, his finger hovering over a series of photographs that depicted grim scenes from previous cases.

"Anesh's father is using locations we're already familiar with," he explained, his tone grave yet focused.

"He used the cabin to kill my father. It means…" Ishank trailed off, realization dawning upon him like a dark cloud gathering before a storm.

"It means, Ishank," Ronak interjected sharply, "that he will choose a place associated with past traumas! A location steeped in fear and memories!"

One of the officers chimed in hesitantly, "He might have kept Ruhi's family at their home."

Ronak shook his head vehemently. "No! He will never do that. He thrives on psychological torment. He's only using places tied to their past traumas."

"Sandy at the fields… Ruhi at that abandoned building…" Ishank murmured, piecing together the horrific jigsaw.

"Correct!" Ronak affirmed, his voice rising with urgency. "But we still don't know where he could have kept your mother. We must check that swimming pool where Anesh killed Samaira."

"I'll take care of it," Ankit said resolutely.

"Jatin and Sakshi," Ronak instructed sharply, "you two head for that abandoned building. Ankit, you go to the swimming pool where Samaira died—take local police with you! Now hurry!"

The officers nodded briskly before darting out into the night like arrows released from a bow.

"Ishank," Ronak said softly but firmly as he turned back to him, "I need you here. Think about all possible places where he might have kept your mother. Don't lose courage; we will find them all." His eyes bore into Ishank's with an intensity that conveyed both reassurance and urgency.

"I want you to be strong and stay in touch with your dad," Ronak continued, his voice steady despite the chaos around them. "I'm going to check out the fields where Sandy died."

As Ronak left, Ishank felt a mixture of gratitude and fear swell within him. The weight of uncertainty pressed heavily on his chest as he stood alone in the dimly lit room filled with evidence boards and scattered files—a silent witness to their desperate race against time.

He closed his eyes for a moment, summoning every ounce of strength within him. The stakes were high; lives hung in balance. With each tick of the clock echoing ominously in his ears, he knew they had to act fast before darkness swallowed them whole once again.

About three and a half hours later, Ishank's phone buzzed insistently, pulling him from the fog of despair that had settled over him. He glanced at the screen and saw Ronak's name flashing. With a shaky breath, he answered, his heart racing in anticipation.

"Ishank! Ruhi is safe!" Ronak's voice burst through the line, a mix of urgency and relief. "Jatin and Sakshi found her unconscious in that abandoned building. We've secured the place just in time—he was going to burn her alive! And there's more good news: we also rescued Ruhi's parents from the fields. But…" Ronak hesitated, the weight of his next words palpable even over the phone. "We have no trace of your mother. Have you figured out anything?"

A wave of conflicting emotions crashed over Ishank—joy for Ruhi's family mingled with a deep, gnawing sadness for his own. His voice trembled as he replied, "No, sir, I haven't. I can't think straight. I don't know what to do." Desperation clawed at him, each word heavy with the burden of his failure.

"Don't worry, Ishank," Ronak reassured him, though his tone was laced with concern. "We will find a way."

Just then, Ishank's phone chimed again—a notification for a video call link. He felt a chill run down his spine as he recognized the urgency in its timing.

"Ronak, I need to call you back," Ishank said quickly, anxiety bubbling beneath his calm facade.

He ended the call and clicked on the link. The screen flickered to life, revealing Anesh's father, his face taut with worry against a backdrop of green that looked almost like a curtain drawn tightly across his grief.

"I guess Ruhi's family has been saved by some mighty friends of yours," Anesh's father began, his voice dripping with sarcasm that barely masked his anguish. "But what about your mother? You left her to die with only an hour to spare! Your one decision could've saved your family, Ishank. Instead, you chose to play savior for those you barely know."

Ishank felt a surge of guilt wash over him; it was as if Anesh's father had reached through the screen and gripped his heart in a vice.

"I'm giving you a chance," Anesh's father continued, his eyes narrowing as if he were weighing Ishank's soul. "You can still save your mother by…"

"By what?" Ishank interrupted, desperation creeping into his voice.

"You have to sacrifice yourself," Anesh's father said coldly. "Go to the same cliff where you killed my son. Jump from that cliff. You have one hour, Ishank. Time is running out for your mother." He leaned back slightly, the green curtain behind him seeming to close in like a noose tightening around Ishank's throat. "Signing off."

The call ended abruptly, leaving Ishank staring at the screen in disbelief as silence enveloped him like a shroud. The weight of Anesh's father's words hung heavy in the air—sacrifice himself? The thought sent shivers down his spine.

With no time to waste and dread pooling in his stomach like lead, Ishank bolted from his seat and raced toward the cliff—a place haunted by memories and regrets. The wind whipped through his hair as he drove through the desolate landscape; trees blurred past like ghosts whispering warnings.

Thirty minutes later, he arrived at the cliff's edge, breathless and trembling. The sun hung low in the sky, casting an orange glow that danced ominously on the horizon—a beautiful yet cruel backdrop for what lay ahead.

His phone buzzed incessantly in his pocket; Ronak was trying to reach him again. But Ishank couldn't bear to answer it now—not when every ring felt like a reminder of everything he stood to lose.

He stepped closer to the edge, peering down into the abyss below—a dark void that seemed to beckon him with promises of peace and escape from this tormenting dilemma. The wind howled around him as if urging him forward or warning him away; it was impossible to tell.

In that moment of solitude and chaos combined, memories flooded back: laughter shared with friends, moments spent with Ruhi before everything spiraled out of control. Each recollection felt like a knife twisting deeper into his heart.

"I can't do this," he whispered to himself, tears blurring his vision as he fought against despair.

But then there was another thought—his mother's face flashed before him: warm smiles and loving embraces now overshadowed by fear for her life. Could he really let her die?

Psychowrath

As he stood there teetering on the brink of decision, Ishank felt a surge of determination rise within him—a flicker of hope amidst despair. He would not let fear dictate his actions any longer.

"I will find another way!" he shouted into the wind defiantly, clenching his fists until they turned white with resolve.

With renewed purpose coursing through him like fire in his veins, Ishank turned away from the cliff's edge, the wind howling around him like a banshee. He pulled out his phone, the device trembling in his grip as he dialed Ronak's number. *I need you now*, he thought desperately. They would figure this out together—he wouldn't let anyone else down again.

As he pressed the call button, hope flickered within him like a candle fighting against the dark—a small but fierce light ready to illuminate even the darkest path ahead.

"Where were you, Ishank? Why haven't you been picking up my calls?" Ronak's voice crackled through the line, laced with urgency and concern.

"I don't have time to explain," Ishank gasped, his heart racing. "He called again. He wants me to die—only then will my mother be saved! I'm near the cliff!" His voice trembled with fear and desperation.

"Listen! Calm down, Ishank!" Ronak urged, his tone shifting to one of steely resolve. "What if he kills your mother after you die? We only have twenty-five minutes! Think! Did you notice anything unusual in his actions? Anything strange?"

Ishank closed his eyes, trying to recall every detail. "Yes… there was a green background when he was talking to me. I don't know what it means."

Ronak's mind raced as he connected the dots. "Ishank, Anesh loved cinema, right? He always dreamed of working in movies and plays."

"Yes, but what does that have to do with any of this?" Ishank replied, confusion mingling with fear.

"I know where he is!" Ronak exclaimed, adrenaline surging through him. "He's at a studio! The college where Anesh studied is closed for vacation. His father must have hired it out; it's the perfect place for him to operate without anyone noticing. The voices you heard—the background of trees—it was all a ruse to confuse us! Ankit is already at the college, and I'll reach there in five minutes. I promise you, Ishank—I will save your mother!"

"Please hurry!" Ishank pleaded, tears streaming down his face as panic clawed at his throat.

Psychowrath

Ronak hung up and raced towards the college with Ankit by his side. The clock was ticking ominously; they had only ten minutes left.

As they approached the studio, shadows danced across the walls under flickering fluorescent lights. The air was thick with tension and uncertainty—the kind that made every footfall feel like a countdown to disaster.

Suddenly, they spotted movement inside one of the rooms. It was Anesh's father, lurking like a predator waiting for its prey. Ronak's heart pounded as he grabbed him from behind, pinning him against the wall with fierce determination.

"Where have you kept Ishank's mother? Tell us now!" Ronak demanded, his voice low and menacing.

Anesh's father turned slowly, a monstrous smile spreading across his face like a dark omen. "Boom," he laughed maniacally, sending chills down their spines.

"Oh my God!" Ankit gasped, eyes wide with horror. "He has tied Ishank's mother to a bomb! We need to disarm it—he must have a remote here! Find it fast!"

Ronak quickly handcuffed Anesh's father, who squirmed in protest but was no match for Ronak's resolve. Time was slipping away; they had only three minutes left.

"Check his pockets!" Ronak shouted at Ankit as he rifled through the man's belongings. His heart raced as he felt something cold and metallic—a remote control!

With shaking hands, Ronak pressed the off button on the remote, praying for a miracle. The seconds stretched into an eternity as he held his breath—then relief washed over him like a wave: *the bomb was disarmed.* Ishank's mother was safe.

Ronak quickly dialed Ishank's number, urgency lacing his voice. "Ishank! She is safe—your mother is safe! She's at your house right now. I'm sending a bomb squad with some of my officers there—you need to get there too!"

Tears filled Ishank's eyes as relief flooded over him like a warm embrace. "Thank you so much… thank you very much," he choked out between sobs.

Ronak and Ankit burst out of the studio, adrenaline coursing through their veins like wildfire. The weight of the night's events hung heavy in the air, but Ronak felt a flicker of triumph. He had saved the case without a single life lost—a feat that seemed almost impossible given the circumstances. He had avenged the murder of his dear friend, Mr. Kapoor, whose memory had haunted him since that fateful day.

As they made their way to the precinct, Ronak's mind raced with thoughts of the interrogation to come. Anesh's father was in custody now, and Ronak was determined to extract every ounce of information he could about the other killings committed by his son.

Inside the stark interrogation room, the atmosphere was tense. The fluorescent lights flickered overhead, casting harsh shadows on the walls. Anesh's father sat slumped in his chair, his eyes hollow and filled with despair. Ronak leaned forward, his voice steady yet firm.

"Let's talk about Anesh," he began, watching for any sign of resistance. "We know he didn't act alone in the murders of Samaira and Sandy. You were with him, weren't you?"

Anesh's father looked up sharply, a mixture of anger and sorrow etched across his face. "Do you think Anesh managed all that alone?" he spat, his voice rising. "He never got caught because I was there with him every single time! Your police couldn't trace his fingerprints at the murder scenes because I carefully planned everything!"

Ronak felt a chill run down his spine as he listened to the man's confession. It was a twisted bond between father and son—one built on crime and deceit.

"Why did you do it?" Ronak pressed, his heart racing. "What drove you to help him kill those innocent people?"

Anesh's father paused, tears streaming down his cheeks as he struggled to find words amidst his grief. "After his mother died when he was just ten," he said, voice cracking with emotion, "I raised him with everything I could do for him. He was a brilliant student—a talented person who excelled in both studies and extracurricular activities."

The room fell silent as he continued, his voice barely above a whisper. "What was his mistake? Huh? That he loved a girl? He came to me sobbing and panting after throwing Ishank from that cliff that day. He was scared… scared of losing everything."

Ronak felt a pang of sympathy for Anesh's father despite the horror of what he had done. The man had lost so much—yet it didn't excuse his actions.

"I instructed him on what to do next," Anesh's father continued, anguish twisting his features. "But life was so cruel to him! He faced so many obstacles in the years to come—Samaira… Sandy… Ruhi… and then your dear friend Mr. Kapoor." His voice broke as he recalled the tragedies that had befallen them.

"And when he was killed," he added bitterly, "he told me nothing! I was out of the city when you monsters killed my child! You didn't even spare his unborn child!" His voice rose in pitch as rage consumed him.

In court, Anesh's father received a life sentence for his crimes. However, after careful observation of his actions during the trial, the judge ordered him to be placed in a psychiatric asylum for treatment—a decision that left many feeling uneasy about what might happen next.

Meanwhile, Ishank and Ruhi's families finally found solace after years of turmoil and fear. The weight of their shared grief began to lift as they embraced new beginnings.

Ishank took charge of his father's sneaker business— a venture that had been passed down through generations. The once-familiar smell of leather and rubber filled the air as he walked through the bustling factory floor, where workers chatted amicably while assembling shoes with nimble fingers.

In those months following the chaos, Ishank and Ruhi discovered something beautiful amidst their pain: love blossomed like a flower breaking through concrete. Their connection deepened as they navigated their healing journeys together—sharing laughter over coffee dates and quiet evenings spent watching movies under a blanket fort made from old sheets.

One evening, as they strolled hand-in-hand through a vibrant market filled with colors and sounds that danced around them like music, Ishank paused beneath a canopy of twinkling lights. He turned to Ruhi, heart racing with anticipation.

"Ruhi," he said softly, searching her eyes for encouragement. "I want to spend my life with you."

Ruhi's breath hitched as she realized what he meant; her heart swelled with joy at the thought of forever with him.

With their families' blessings echoing in their hearts, Ishank and Ruhi exchanged vows six months later in an intimate ceremony surrounded by loved ones who had supported them through thick and thin.

As they settled into their new life in Chandigarh after their wedding—decorating their cozy apartment with laughter and love—the couple felt an overwhelming sense of peace enveloping them like a warm embrace.

Two years passed quickly; time seemed to fly by like leaves caught in an autumn breeze. Ishank and Ruhi became parents to a beautiful baby boy whom they named Garvit—a name that meant 'worthy' or 'honored.' Their home echoed with laughter as Garvit took his first steps and uttered sweet words that melted their hearts.

But fate has a way of twisting even the most idyllic stories into nightmares.

On Garvit's second birthday—a day filled with balloons and cake—the unthinkable happened: their precious boy vanished without a trace amidst the joyful chaos of party guests celebrating around them.

Panic ensued as Ishank and Ruhi searched frantically among friends and family members who were oblivious to their growing horror. Time seemed to stretch infinitely as they called out for Garvit again and again until their voices were hoarse from fear.

With Anesh's father locked away in an asylum—his influence seemingly extinguished—who could have committed such an atrocity? As dread settled into their bones like ice water coursing through their veins, Ishank realized they needed help; there was only one person they could turn to—Ronak.

Desperation clawed at them as they reached out to Ronak once more—their last hope in this dark hour.

As Ronak arrived at their home later that evening—
the shadows lengthening ominously around him—he
found Ishank pacing back-and-forth like a caged
animal while Ruhi clutched her husband's arm tightly;
both were pale with fear.

"What happened?" Ronak asked urgently as he took
in their frantic expressions.

"Garvit is missing!" Ishank exclaimed breathlessly,
eyes wild with panic. "He disappeared during his
birthday party! We don't know how it happened!"

Ronak's mind raced; questions flooded through him
like an avalanche: *Who could have done this? Did we miss
something? Is there anyone working for Anesh's father still out
there?*

The atmosphere thickened with uncertainty as they
exchanged worried glances—each person grappling
with their own fears while trying desperately to
remain strong for one another.

The clock ticked ominously in the background—a
reminder that every second counted—and Ronak
knew they needed answers fast before it was too late.

As darkness fell outside like an impenetrable cloak
enveloping them all in its grasp—one thing became
painfully clear: this battle was far from over; shadows

from their past were creeping back into their lives once more.

Months passed, each day dragging on like a heavy fog that refused to lift. The sun rose and set, but for Ishank and Ruhi, time had lost its meaning. Garvit's absence was a gaping hole in their lives, an emptiness that echoed with every heartbeat. Ronak, their unwavering ally, devoted himself to finding Garvit, but every lead turned cold like the winter air that seeped into their bones.

Ronak poured over surveillance footage from every corner of the city, scrutinizing the faces of passersby with a relentless intensity. He combed through records of known criminals involved in kidnapping and extortion, but nothing surfaced. Each day felt like a futile battle against an unseen enemy, and the weight of despair pressed down on him like a heavy shroud.

In a desperate attempt to bring Garvit home, Ishank made a bold announcement: a cash prize of 25 lakhs for anyone who could provide information leading to his son's safe return. The news spread like wildfire through the community—a flicker of hope amidst the darkness. But as the weeks turned into months, that hope began to wane.

The once-vibrant home they had decorated for Garvit's second birthday now stood in stark contrast to their grief. The balloons that had floated cheerfully above the living room were deflated and forgotten, gathering dust in the corners. The cake they had ordered sat untouched in the fridge—a bittersweet reminder of what should have been. Ishank and Ruhi had lost interest in everything; their laughter replaced by silence that echoed through the halls.

Six months passed without a single day where they smiled or found solace in each other's company. Friends and family tried to reach out, offering support and encouragement, but their words fell flat against the overwhelming sorrow that engulfed them. Everyone around them began to lose hope that Garvit would ever return—everyone except Ishank.

Determined not to give up on his son, Ishank became a man possessed by purpose. He plastered advertisements across town with Garvit's picture—his bright eyes and cheeky smile staring back at anyone who would look. He contacted private investigators, walked the streets with flyers clutched tightly in his hands, asking everyone he encountered if they had seen his boy.

"Have you seen him?" he would plead with strangers, desperation lacing his voice. "Please! He's just two years old!"

Psychowrath

Each rejection felt like a dagger to his heart, but he pressed on—driven by love and an unyielding belief that Garvit was still out there somewhere.

As another six months slipped by, the calendar marked Garvit's third birthday—a day that should have been filled with joy and celebration but now loomed like a dark cloud overhead. Despite the heaviness in his heart, Ishank resolved to decorate their home for Garvit's birthday; it was a small act of defiance against despair. Balloons were inflated once more, streamers hung from the ceiling, and a small cake was placed on the table—an offering to the universe in hopes that it would bring his son back.

That evening, as twilight descended upon the city and stars began to twinkle overhead like distant memories of happier times, Ishank received an unexpected notification on his phone—a video from an unknown source.

His heart raced as he opened it, anticipation mingling with dread. The screen flickered to life, revealing Garvit's familiar face—his cherubic features twisted in distress as he called out for his dad through tears. Behind him was a television broadcasting the latest news of the present date.

"Dad! Help me!" Garvit cried, his voice trembling with fear.

Ishank felt his heart shatter into a million pieces at the sight of his son suffering. "Garvit!" he shouted into the phone, desperation clawing at his throat as he reached out toward the screen as if he could pull his boy back through it.

But then came a voice—cold and sinister—that sent chills racing down Ishank's spine. "Happy to see your toddler," it said mockingly. "But you won't be able to see him if you don't fulfill what I demand."

Ishank's breath caught in his throat as he listened intently. The voice continued, dripping with malice. "I will send something soon containing details of what has to be done. And listen carefully: if police get involved in this case… your boy will be dead the next moment."

The video ended abruptly, leaving Ishank staring at his phone in shock—the weight of those words crashing down on him like a tidal wave. He felt sick; panic surged through him as he struggled to process what had just happened.

"Who is this person?" he muttered under his breath, anger boiling beneath the surface. "Why are they doing this?"

Ruhi rushed into the room at that moment, her eyes wide with concern as she sensed something was wrong. "Ishank? What happened? You look pale!"

He turned to her, anguish etched across his face as he recounted what he had just seen and heard—the video of Garvit calling for help and the chilling ultimatum from whoever held their son captive.

Ruhi gasped, covering her mouth with trembling hands as tears filled her eyes. "No… no! This can't be happening!" She sank onto the couch, burying her face in her hands as sobs wracked her body.

"I won't let them take him from us again," Ishank vowed fiercely, determination igniting within him like a flame rekindled after being extinguished for too long. "We have to figure out what they want."

As they sat together on that couch—two broken souls united by love and desperation—their thoughts raced with questions:

Who was this mysterious figure? What did they want from them? Why now?

The shadows danced around them as night fell outside—a reminder that darkness often hides secrets waiting to be uncovered.

With every passing moment, time slipped away like sand through their fingers; they knew they were running out of it fast.

As Ishank held Ruhi close—both terrified yet resolute—they prepared themselves for whatever lay ahead; they were determined not only to find Garvit but also to confront whatever sinister forces were at play in this twisted game.

Stay tuned for the next chapter in Ishank and his family's journey, where old memories resurface, new alliances form, and the stakes rise higher than ever.

Coming soon: *Psychowrath: The Reckoning.*

—The End—

Acknowledgements

First and foremost, I extend my deepest gratitude to my family. Your unwavering faith in my capabilities and ceaseless encouragement were my pillars of strength throughout this endeavor. I am truly blessed to have such a supportive and loving family.

To my friends, thank you for being my sounding board, for the laughter in between the stressful moments, and for always being there when I needed a pick-me-up. Your friendship and support are immeasurable.

My heartfelt appreciation goes to all my readers and followers. Each word of encouragement, every constructive criticism will help me grow as a writer, and for that, I am eternally grateful.

A special thanks to the team at Notion Press for their guidance and professionalism, and for making the publishing process a smooth and enjoyable experience.

Finally, I extend my gratitude to all those who have indirectly contributed to this project, knowingly or unknowingly. The world is a constant source of inspiration, and I am ever grateful for the experiences that have led me to this point.

Writing this book has been an incredible journey, and I am grateful to have shared it with all of you.